I0457440

Coming Full Circle

FOLLOWING THE PATH
WITH HEART

Coming Full Circle
FOLLOWING THE PATH
WITH HEART

Toni Tarango

Coming Full Circle: Following the Path With Heart
by Toni Tarango

© 2024 Toni Tarango
Published by Plumbum Press
Oakland, CA

All Rights Reserved

The right of Toni Tarango to be identified as the author of this work has been asserted by her in accordance with the copyright laws.

No part of this publication may be reproduced, transmitted, or stored in a retrieval system, in any form or by any means, without permission in writing from the copyright holder.

Any similarity to actual persons, living or dead, or actual events, is purely coincidental.

ISBN: 979-8-9889721-4-3 (Paperback)

Our stories help us to better understand ourselves and our reality, because they create the potential for emotions and a scope of possibility that extends far beyond what our day-to-day lives will allow. In doing so, they create a web of relationships that allow us to see beyond the ordinary horizon. Our visions are the shoulders we stand upon to see over the land of possibility.

~ Thomas T. Hills, Ph.D., Professor of Psychology, University of Warwick, England

A special thanks to longtime friend and graphic designer Chris Molé.
Your creativity and attention to detail on the covers for *Coming Full Circle* and *As the Eagle Soars* have been such a gift.
Who knew that I'd have to wait two decades before finding out first-hand how talented you are as a book designer. #ChrisMoleDesign

Contents

Special Dedication

First and foremost, I want to acknowledge the efforts of Indigenous Elders and Culture Keepers throughout the North American continent. These individuals are the primary teachers within their communities. Elders and Culture Keepers are vital to the preservation of customs, knowledge, and traditions specific to the origins of their tribes. This is an enormously important and sacred task and one that I believe to be of extreme significance for both the Indigenous and non-Indigenous populations living on this planet.

> *"As early as the 1830s, it was widely assumed that Native Americans were facing extermination. But the predictions were wrong. Entering the 20th century, Native American numbers began to rise. The upturn was gradual at first, but by 1990 the survival of Native North Americans was indisputable. This long, slow recovery to some seemed almost a fulfillment of the refrain in a century-old Comanche Ghost Dance song: We shall live again; we shall live again."*
>
> ~ *Through Indian Eyes: The Untold Story of Native American Peoples*, Pg. 353.

Today there are 574 federally recognized tribes in the USA, though there were likely to have been hundreds, if not thousands more throughout the history of the continent.

Preface

Around 2003, I took an introduction to fiction writing class at Berkeley City College in Berkeley, California. The framework for the original short story came from a personal conflict that occurred every time I filled out an employment application and was asked about "ethnicity and race." My father, Raul Flores Tarango (RIP 3/2019) was Mexican American and my mother, Sally Elaine Nave (RIP 1/2023) was of European descent. At that time, employment applications didn't have a "bicultural" box, and I often felt guilty checking the box for "Hispanic" or "Latino", because I didn't look the part. Plus, my last name was frequently thought to be Italian, which didn't help matters. However, the job application dilemma got me thinking about how, at a deeper level, this might also be an issue for others, and that led to the extended version of this original short story. So, therein lies the genesis of this creation!

Decades ago, I had the privilege of working with Pima dialysis patients in a social services capacity. These individuals were members of the Gila River Indian Reservation aka Sacaton, located south of Chandler, AZ. I want to be clear that I do not claim to be an authority on Native American customs, or traditions. The gatherings I describe in this story are not affiliated with the above-mentioned tribe. *The Between Two Worlds trilogy: 1) As the Twig is Bent-Between Two Worlds, 2) As the Eagle Soars-At Birth and Beyond,* and *3) Coming Full Circle* are works of fiction and in no way claim to document any indigenous custom or tradition with any degree of authority.

Toni Tarango
Author

CHAPTER 1

The Way of Wisdom

"Wisdom is the part of spiritual intelligence that allows us to see people and situations with clarity, as well as a natural understanding of the relationship between seemingly unrelated things."

~ Doug Good Feather, from *Think Indigenous*

As I sit on our front porch, the view of the desert mountains is lovely. In mid-November the weather is mild, and the winds are cool. As I settle into this rocking chair, I hear the squeaking of the old wood. Shortly after my Nykwr'ak (husband), found out I was pregnant, he got busy making what he called Mama's rocker. Now, Mama's rocker is worn, having soothed two crying babies and lulling them to sleep long ago. Not only this chair, but the adobe style home we had built all those years ago has stood the test of time and protected our growing family from the harsh desert sun and open winds. As I feel my bones creaking, like my rocker, I can look back and see the truth of my journey.

After the death of my brother Keith, I knew I needed to rediscover myself. I had to find out who I was as a freestanding woman, but not an unattached woman. I took a new path, an unfamiliar journey into my indigenous ancestry to a richer and more diverse existence. This new life had its challenges, and I was prodded and tested in ways I never could have imagined.

The Joslin Gentry of my youth was timid and hid behind books and her brother; however, I'd finally emerged from my cocoon as a fully formed butterfly. In honor of my personal transformation and my generational gift, Grandma Moon gave me the name of "Butterfly Woman", which means a healer with a strong connection to dream spirits. I was still an ever-talented craftsperson, which complimented my primary role on Nagchaw.

As the Director of the Nagchaw Cultural Center, I oversaw a broad range of programming related to the preservation of the Nagchaw culture and traditions. We had displays showcasing the art of basketry, pottery, weaving, and other traditional crafts. There were two language classes taught by Lucy Keeton who was reintroducing the Nagchaw River People's dialect, or Uto-Aztecan language. One class was for adults, those who'd grown up speaking the language. This class was more about creating a sense of community that allowed these adults to sharpen and show off their language skills. The second class was for young people who'd heard the language but only knew a few words. Each quarter, the two classes would meet for a potluck and skill building conversations. At this gathering, the students were asked to pair off between the classes and could only speak to each other using the River People's dialect. At the end of the potluck the pairs presented what their experiences were while conversing with one another. With full bellies and lots of laughter, this was always the most popular class!

I took on an advocacy role with the Nagchaw youth (13-19) related to understanding their rights in the white man's world. By way of guest speakers, the curriculum allowed for presentations from tribal mainstays, like Mike Milton from the Thunder Road Recovery program, our Medical Social Worker Adriane Willis on suicide prevention, as well as Officer's Dakoda and Montera representing the Nagchaw P.D. In addition, there were speakers from First Nation advocacy agencies traveling primarily from Tucson to speak about scams, sex trafficking, gangs, and other crimes. In addition, there were representatives from employment training programs and educational institutions like Job Corps, Desert Sage Community College, and the University of Arizona who spoke about educational grants, and available internships.

After Keith's passing, Jericho Jefferson decided to stay on for another year as the Tribal Council Chief Executive. A couple of months after the funeral, Stevie Bahe came to Jericho asking to do an internship so that he could run the next time a council seat opened. Stevie received valuable tutelage from Jericho, and as fate would have it, the next seat that opened was Jericho's. Stevie ran an outstanding campaign and was elected by a landslide as the next Tribal Council Chief Executive. At his induction ceremony, he addressed the loss of Keith and reflected a deep understanding of what that loss meant to the Nagchaw Nation. In his closing comments, Stevie committed himself to follow the examples set by Jericho Jefferson and Keith Gentry.

Keith would have wholeheartedly approved of Stevie Bahe's election to Jericho's seat. Stevie had been a year behind Keith and a couple years ahead of me at Coleman High, but they'd run track together. Keith knew him to be not only a formidable opponent but trustworthy and proud of his ancestry.

When the results came back from Jericho and Keith's paternity test, he announced this news to the Nagchaw Nation by way of a Special Edition of The Tribal Voice. Jericho acknowledged that the rumors over the years had prompted him to urge Keith to take the paternity test, which my brother willingly agreed to do. He outlined the contributions made by Keith to the Tribal Council and stated that he had come to genuinely love and respect the young man that he always felt was his biological son.

My parents divorced. Sam did a partial sale of Gentry Construction with that out-of-town firm, and they took over running things in Coleman. He lived in our family home while he had a rustic two bedroom, two bath cabin built on the outskirts of Flagstaff. After he moved, our family home was sold. It came as a surprise to us all when Sam gave the full sale amount to my mother, which I believe he did as a gesture of remorse. Was Sam willing to change? Probably not, but I believe he knew that he did not treat my mother well during most of their married life.

We had a traditional adobe-style duplex built near the center of Nagchaw. Grandma Moon and Pawpaw lived on one side and Mom and I on the other, which was convenient as far as getting together for meals, holidays, and other celebrations. It also allowed me to walk to work, which I enjoyed.

Grandma and Mom took to cultivating a large, raised bed garden in the backyard filled with an assortment of herbs, fruit, and veggies. This was the easiest method of gardening in the desert, less time-consuming and did not require tilling. Because it was covered in chicken wire, it kept out those small varmints that normally would have feasted on the garden contents.

Now that we were both living on Nagchaw, Mom and Jericho started seeing each other shortly after he resigned from the tribal council. It's interesting how we cross paths with those who have been and will continue to be significant in our lives.

Life was full, and I was getting attention from

different men on the reservation. My mother had once described herself to me as being "very inexperienced" when it came to men. After all, her experience was limited to Jericho Jefferson and Sam Gentry. Unlike my mother, I'd never really had a serious long-term relationship. I'd had secret crushes on a handful of guys in high school. I went out with a couple of them briefly, but nothing much came of it. Given that I had been moved up a grade, in elementary school and again in middle school, it had always been a challenge relating to my peers.

Looking back at those times now, I realize how I was affected by my parents' relationship. Sam was my biological father, and I found him untrustworthy as it related to how he treated my mother. Although he never actually struck me, he left wounds that I needed to address. While in grad school, I started seeing a family therapist. Those weekly sessions were invaluable. I now understood much more about how my personal history came to influence my attitudes and behavior as an adult.

Still, as much as I'd love to have a family, I must admit that I hadn't fully resolved my intimacy issues. Having Keith and Sam as examples of what being a man meant, was like having two angels, a good and a bad one on each shoulder. Could I trust that I'd end up listening to the good angel? Given my luck, I'd probably end up listening to the bad angel. It scared me to think about it, so I avoided those men interested in becoming more than friends.

CHAPTER 2

Reaching the Finish Line

"Genuine beginnings depend upon a kind of inner realignment rather than on external shifts, for when we are aligned with deep longings, we become powerfully motivated."

~ William Bridges, from *Transitions: Making Sense of Life's Changes*

It was hard to believe that it had been so many years since the Nagchaw Nation received word about the untimely death of my brother, Keith. After Keith's funeral the Nagchaw PD moved forward with investigating the hit and run.

That individual was found to be none other than my brother's high school nemesis, Jack Mitchell. Not only had Jack left the scene of the fatal accident, but he'd fled once the Nagchaw and Coleman police started looking for him. Eventually, Jack was arrested in Kingman on his way to Las Vegas and was returned to the area to stand trial.

The first piece of evidence was the anonymous phone call reporting the accident, which was voice analyzed and identified as Jack's voice. Secondly, the black and red paint damage on the driver's side of Keith's truck matched perfectly to the front-end damage on Jack's truck. And, finally, the proverbial nail in the coffin was Jack's inebriated boasting about the hit and run to anyone who'd listen at The 5th Amendment Bar. It left everyone surprised that the trial lasted as long as it did.

The trial was held at the Pima County Superior Court in Tucson. The presiding Judge, the Honorable Newman Archibald, had a reputation for being strictly by the book, especially with criminal hit and run cases. Judge Archibald did not go lightly on Jack Mitchell's defense team either. These unscrupulous mouthpieces had reputations for unprofessional behavior, everything from failing to show up for meetings, filing paperwork incorrectly, and occasionally missing deadlines.

On the final day of the trial, the entire Nagchaw Nation was present to hear the verdict announced. I sat in front with my mother, Jericho Jefferson, Grandma Moon, Pawpaw, Telrica, and Mike Milton. I felt the strength of my immediate circle. I knew that no matter the outcome those closest to me would always honor and uphold the memory of my brother.

Upon hearing the verdict, those present erupted as cheering echoed throughout the Superior Court building! This felony hit and run got Jack Mitchell a ten-year-prison sentence, a $5,000 fine, and his license revoked. The fine was donated to the Nagchaw Cultural Center's

Understanding Your Rights program in Keith's name.

The week after the trial ended was the one-year anniversary of Keith's passing. At the request of Mom, Grandma Moon and Pawpaw, the Tribal Council and the Council of Elders approved holding a traditional Nagchaw burial on the reservation. It was as my brother would have wanted.

Keith's body had already been buried, so a mock body was made of straw, cloth, and other natural materials by Mom and Grandma Moon. They dressed the figure in one of Keith's ceremonial, ribbon shirts and a ceremonial mask.

On Saturday evening, Mom and Jericho went through a mock ritual cleansing of the body and preparing it for burial. At sunrise on Sunday, the mock body was placed on a special woven mat made by Telrica. Then the woven mat with the mock body was laid on top of a funeral pyre which had been erected by Mike Milton and Stevie Bahe. This way Keith's body would pass from this life to the great bonfire in the afterlife, assuring his return by way of reincarnation. While Pawpaw proceeded with the burial blessing and songs, the Thunder Road men's group began drumming. As the flames consumed the mock body signifying the release of Keith's spirit, one of the drummers pointed to the sky with his mallet. As everyone looked upward, a large brown eagle circled above the gathering. Souls of esteemed warriors are escorted to the Great Beyond by a brown eagle. Keith's spirit was being escorted into the heavens as the Nagchaw Nation mourned, again.

Later that afternoon, The Tribal Council held a luncheon to honor Keith. Lucy Keeton and several other women on the reservation prepared a wide assortment of traditional dishes, and all were invited to share a midday meal together. The gathering was festive in nature, and many of those attending shared poignant and humorous stories about encounters with Keith; several people said that they felt Keith's spirit was present at the luncheon. As the afternoon wined down, Jericho Jefferson got up to say a few words.

"As a family the Nagchaw Nation stands together in remembering our departed son, brother, friend, and warrior. As much as Keith's mother and I ache to have him with us, we know that Keith resides with our ancestors, The Nagchaw Ancients. We feel his presence amongst us during this time, and we rejoice in celebrating what his life had been. As the son I never knew until the last two years of his life, I am grateful to have had that time with him. He was a man I am proud to call my son. He will be cherished in my heart, as well as his families' hearts forever. Thank you all for coming,"

Jericho closed the luncheon with tears in his eyes.

After the luncheon was over, Telrica and I stayed to help Lucy Keeton, and the Tribal Council staff, Rachel, and Allie with the cleanup. There wasn't much food left over, but enough to feed a couple of elders for two, maybe three days. We'd wrapped up the leftovers and gave them to Grandma Moon and Pawpaw to take home. Both expressed their appreciativeness and where happy to have the assortment of traditional foods for later.

"Oh, thank you, Granddaughter. This will certainly help keep your grandfather from blowing away in the wind," Grandma said laughing as she lovingly smiled at Pawpaw.

They left the building with Jericho and Mom to walk home. I continued with the cleanup. When Lucy, Allie, and Rachel finished, they said their goodbyes and headed home. Suddenly, as Telrica and I were about to leave, a noticeable wind blew through the building. There were no doors or windows open, and the air conditioning had been turned off. The strange wind gust brought an electrified presence. Telrica and I stopped.

"Sisters, although I am no longer with you on the physical plane, I am with you in spirit and will watch over you throughout your lives. We are now as we have always been, linked to the web of life. I crossed the Great

River and what needed to happen for each of you has happened; therefore, my primordial task at this juncture has been fulfilled. Ny'thkvekuum."

"Did you hear that?! 'Ny'thkvekuum' means he's going home," I said.

"Yes, I heard him. I'm so glad that he's watching over us, Jos. That means we can talk with him whenever we feel the need. He's still the love of my life even as he's crossed the Great River," Telrica said.

With the trial ended and the traditional ceremony, it felt a step closer to closure. I say a step, because there would be no quick closing to the significant life that had been my beloved brother. Even so, especially with his spirit message after the luncheon, I felt more at peace than I had since his death occurred. I very much sensed it was the same with Mom, Jericho, Grandma Moon, and Pawpaw.

Pawpaw had been greatly affected by Keith's passing, and Grandma and Mom had been worried about him. Interestingly, having Jericho around to converse with seemed to partially fill the void that Keith's death created. Their bond grew, especially after Jericho's special announcement in the Nagchaw Tribal Voice. Having validated that Keith was in fact Jericho Jefferson's biological son seemed to make both men supremely happy. In fact, once the announcement was made from that point forward, my brother was referred to as Keith Jefferson on the reservation.

Together Jericho and Pawpaw designed a new headstone that replaced the one at the Coleman Cemetery. This new headstone was a rich, sand-colored marble and had a large soaring brown eagle laser etched at the top. The inscription read 'Keith Jefferson, our beloved son, brother, and Nagchaw warrior was called home by The Nagchaw Ancients on 11-05-1982.' The Tribal Voice ran a full front-page story with color pictures of the new headstone at the Coleman Cemetery.

"Nyavee (wife), I will frame this page from the Tribal Voice and hang it on the wall next to our altar. My grandson was a blessing to the Nagchaw Nation, and he will remain in my heart until the day I return to the Great Beyond," Pawpaw said.

"Yes, Nykwr'ak (husband), your relationship with our grandson was special. I know he looked up to you and was so grateful to have you in his life," Grandma Moon said.

"I'm telling you Nyavee (wife), it was an honor to call him grandson. I had to step in and do what I could. After all, Sam ignored Keith and treated him like an outsider. Even though it turned out that our grandson wasn't Sam's biological son, that was no good reason to treat our grandson so coldly. I made sure Keith knew that he was loved and was one of us. It will always be the greatest joy of my life to have been his Nkwo (grandfather) as well as the father figure that Sam chose not to be," Pawpaw said.

CHAPTER 3

Life on the Rez

"The outer forms of our lives can change in an instant, but the inner reorientation that brings us back into a vital relation to people and activity takes time."

~ William Bridges, from Transitions: Making Sense of Life's Changes

The Rez was a rural setting and sparsely populated compared to Coleman. There was no noise pollution and annoying traffic. There were no buildings over two stories, and the atmosphere was laid back, which I had come to relish. Those living on the Rez knew each other, as well as their families and clan histories. They were always willing to lend a hand. Although there was a convenience store and gas station at the main entrance of Nagchaw, there was only one small grocery. Rez families ate homemade meals, used raw milk when pasteurized wasn't available, and had plenty of yardbird eggs. Fresh fruit and vegetables, however, were hard to come by. For a well-stocked grocery store, you had to travel 10 miles into Coleman. This was something that did eventually change. A well-known Arizona grocer,

Bashas', took over the small Rez grocery store and expanded the building, doubling its size, thanks to the diligent work of Stevie Bahe and the Tribal Council.

Originally a small town, Coleman was growing and had certain conveniences—more than one restaurant, a city library, a movie theater, a small park, and high school sports. Coleman had their annual fund-raising bazaar for Saint Mary's, a 4th of July celebration with fireworks, and the Pima County fair, which was held at the fairgrounds in Tucson. I always looked forward to the concerts. Every year I crossed my fingers in the hopes that Carlos Santana, Linda Ronstadt, or The Eagles would perform.

By the 1990's Coleman had experienced exponential growth, so much so that a new shopping venue opened in the downtown area. The new mall offered the convenience of shopping locally and it kept the money in Coleman. The City Center Mall had a J.C. Penny's, a Bashas' grocery store, Walgreen's, an All About Hair Salon, a Books Unlimited, a Hallmark Store, Mrs. Fields Cookies, and Baskin-Robbins Ice Cream. It was also a viable source of employment for residents. Most of the stores had an agreement with the Nagchaw Tribal Council and took on participants from the Rez employment training program. Once participants successfully passed the OJT portion, they were given the option to continue as full-time or part-time employees, which was a decision that most were happy to make.

Stevie Bahe, the Tribal Council Chief Executive, and I had walked to Naturally Native Café for lunch. Afterwards, while heading back to the office, our conversation was revealing. He seemed to be in deep thought, and I wondered what about. From what Keith had told me about Stevie, he was a deep thinker. He reminded my brother of Mike Milton in that way.

"Hey, Jos, how's your mom doing? I've seen her and Jericho at Naturally Native a few times since she's back on the Rez and he's retired. It seems that there's still something between them, yeah?"

"I'm so happy she's seeing Jericho again. He not only respects her, but he also thinks she's beautiful. She's not been with anyone who's really appreciated her in a long time. Jericho seems to still have feelings for her after all this time. His attention is good for her, and I hope it continues."

"So, what about you Jos? Are you seeing anyone these days?"

"Hey now! That's kind of personal, don't you think?" I said giving him that piercing look that I used to give Keith when his questions got too personal.

"Is it? Well then, you tell me. How do I find out if you're seeing anyone? Do I need to put an ear to the Rez rumor mill, or do I get it straight from you? It's your call."

Now, this was the straight-shooting Stevie Bahe that Keith knew and respected. I couldn't really be offended by his question. My reaction was more about my being standoffish where my personal life was concerned. Although I understand why that is now, it's still a pattern I have where men are concerned.

"Okay, you're right. It's best to just ask. Who knows what the rumor mill is saying about me?!"

"Well, if you really want to know, I can tell you," Stevie said chuckling.

"What? Stevie Bahe, are you telling me that there's something going around about me?" I said more than slightly surprised.

"Yes, do you want to know what I've heard?"

"Sure, why not. It's probably something ridiculous or halfway crazy."

"Okay, remember you asked me to tell you," Stevie said.

"Alright Stevie, tell me. I promise I won't slug you too hard," I said laughing too.

"Jos, apparently, you and I are a match made in heaven," Stevie said blushing.

I froze. I was uncomfortable with compliments, and I did everything I could to avoid getting attention from men. Although I understand why that is now, I hated that I still reacted that way.

"Really, so we're an item? Is there anything else you're just dying to tell me?"

"Nope, that's it. We're an item and the Rez thinks it's good medicine. So, I was wondering if we should investigate the rumor to see if there's anything to it," Stevie said smiling.

"What exactly are you suggesting?"

"Well, we could go to dinner in Coleman. Are you familiar with Matta's on Main Street? They've got the best Mexican food around."

"Keith and I loved Matta's. Sure, why not, let's go to dinner sometime."

"Great, if you're free, how about Saturday evening? That's when their Mariachi trio plays."

"This Saturday, so soon?" I said surprised. "Oh boy, you're going to be a tough one. Then you tell me Jos, when are you available to go to dinner," Stevie said.

"Sorry, I don't mean to be difficult. Can I check my calendar and get back to you tomorrow?"

"Sure Jos, let me know tomorrow, or the next day, or by Friday, how's that?" Stevie said.

Stevie was not unlike Keith as far as attracting the attention of women. After all he was quite attractive, a real head turner as the saying goes. In addition, his position required that he be well informed, and aware of the needs of others. From what I could tell, he was also thoughtful, compassionate, and had a great sense of humor. Most importantly, he had the same burning desire that Keith had to make the Nagchaw Nation a better place. And, he was single, or so it had been casually mentioned to me by Lucy Keeton on more than one occasion. So why not go to dinner with him?

Still, I was surprised by his show of interest. Since we'd started working in the same building, he was all about business. Other than occasionally coming downstairs to bring me a cup of coffee and check in, he was very professional and business like. The Tribal Council Chief Executive was my supervisor on paper; however, the reality was that I was free to set my own agenda and create programs or events as I wanted. I did a semiannual report that outlined the activities for the center's calendar, and I was only required to attend the first council staff meeting of each month. At that staff meeting, I gave an update on anything the council needed to know or required their participation, which suited me just fine. The week before my semiannual report was due, I met with Stevie to discuss the center's budget and my need for speaker stipends and other programming expenses. Although we saw each other daily and spoke briefly, we didn't have a lot of in-depth contact other than the above-mentioned. I was normally at work by 8 am and left at 5, while Stevie and his council staff didn't roll in until 9:30 am. He used to tease me that I was making the council look bad, but they did stay until 6:30. This was so they could be available for those returning from work in Coleman should anyone want to meet.

Saturday evening rolled around, and I won't lie, I was nervous. I didn't want to make a big deal out of going to dinner with Stevie, as we were probably only going to do this once. Well, okay, maybe a couple of times as friends, but it certainly wouldn't be more than that.

It took me forever to figure out what to wear. I finally decided on a yellow, three-quarter sleeve, V-neck, cotton blouse with a pair of faded denim capris. I went with my platform sandals since I recently had a pedicure with my favorite nail polish, Totally Toffee. With a final touch of mascara, blush, and a dab of Black Rose oil behind each ear, I was done.

Stevie rolled up in front of our place at 7 pm sharp. I was standing in my bedroom peeking out from behind the curtain's as he got out and walked to the front door. He wore fitted black jeans with a button-down, short sleeve teal cotton shirt, Teva sandals, and his usual wristwatch with a brown leather band. His thick black hair was neatly groomed and pulled back into a ponytail that fell just below his shoulders. Yes, he was an eyecatcher to say the least.

As the little bell on the door knocker jingled, I opened the door.

"Hey, Jos, I hope you're hungry. I've been thinking about Matta's and seeing you all afternoon...okay, not necessarily in that order," Stevie laughed.

"Hi, Stevie, sounds like you're hungry. I'm overdue for my favorite dish, a chili relleno smothered in green sauce," I said blushing from his comment.

As we walked toward his late model, rust colored Chevy El Camino, we both reached for the door handle at the same time. His move to open the car door caught me off guard. I wasn't used to having a door opened for me since Keith's passing.

"Aww, Jos Gentry, I pegged you right. You're going to be a tough one," Stevie said laughing.

"Oh, look Stevie, I'm just not used to having anyone open doors for me, but Keith used to do that. Plus, I'm not helpless you know. I can open a car door for myself, but...it is nice to have someone do that," I said embarrassed about my right off the bat blunder.

"I never doubted that you could, but I'm old school, and it's something I was taught to do. I'd like to do that for you if you'll allow me to."

Stevie opened the car door, and I got in totally embarrassed. I was not happy that this was how our time together started, with me making a thoughtless move right from the onset. I took a deep breath and exhaled as he walked around to the driver's side and got in. Although it was a small thing, it felt big. I started having doubts about having accepted his offer for dinner. I mean, I might regret having done this at some point.

Immediately, I recognized my rush to catastrophic thinking in a personal situation with a male. Uncomfortable circumstances always seemed to carry a heaviness for me because growing up, I had to be careful as making a blunder might result in physical harm.

I told myself to relax because we were going to have a delicious dinner and a great time. Yes, I liked Stevie, and it was going to be okay.

CHAPTER 4

Who is in Charge Here?

"Your decision to evolve consciously through respon-sible choice contributes not only to your evolution, but also to the evolution of all of those aspects of humanity in which you participate. It is not just you that is evolving through your decisions, but the entirety of humanity."

~ Gary Zukav, from *Seat of the Soul*

The Nagchaw Nation was no exception when it came to challenges to social and economic self-reliance. It seemed to me that federal regula-tion and impoverishment went hand in hand. In addition, a significant number of the Nagchaw Nation's women had traumatic histories, which included child abuse, sexual assault, sex traffick-ing, stalking, and other forms of domestic violence.

Being acutely aware of this fact, I began lobby-ing the Tribal Council to work with me on a Rez-wide campaign. By bringing awareness to this issue, it could potentially prevent yet another disheartening statistic in the government's annual BIA report. A significant part of my job was about addressing the here and now of the Nagchaw Nation.

It was Taco Tuesday and Stevie and I had

walked to Naturally Native Café for our weekly lunch together. Emmy Jane took our orders as we talked about the challenges the council faced with the current employment training project. I broached the subject of domestic violence on the Rez to get the ball rolling.

"I can't tackle this issue alone, Stevie. The Elder's Council has already given me their full support. I need the council's backing, which means that they must understand the depth of the issue. Are you hearing me?" I asked.

"I do hear you, but right now is not the best time for the council to tackle another time-consuming issue. We are knee deep in the middle of rolling out the employment training program. You know Jos, this training program is creating a more equitable employment reality for our people," Stevie said.

"I get that, but can we come up with a tentative time for when I can do a presentation to the council? I want their full support and willingness to work with me on a Rez-wide campaign.

"Stevie, it's important to start increasing awareness about domestic violence. Laying the groundwork is key to being able to provide support services for our abused women and children. Now that the Violence Against Women's Act has finally been updated, we need to begin educating our people. They need to understand that now Nagchaw Nation has the legal authority to go after and prosecute criminals, which includes those who commit child abuse and sexual assault. As I see it, that will be one of the central focuses of the Rez-wide campaign. The primary goal will be to bring increased understanding where violence against women and children is concerned. Plus, Adrian Willis, our health center's Licensed Clinical Social Worker has volunteered to put together a recovery program for our women and children."

"Jos, I got you. It is very important. I'll put it on the council's current calendar, and I'll prioritize it at our next staff meeting. Once the employment program gets on its feet, the council will be able to give your presentation their full focus and support, especially the seated council women. Let me look at our timeline calendar when I get back to the office and I'll let you know. I'll also mention this to Captain Batton too. I'm sure he'll want his officers involved in supporting this important issue. In fact, I'll suggest that he come to hear your presentation."

"Excellent idea. Capt. Batton needs to be involved too. Often this abuse isn't reported, but when it is, his officers are the ones who are called to deal with these situations. After he hears my presentation, I'll offer to do a condensed version for his officers at one of his staff meetings."

The preservation of our cultural history and traditions was important, but without addressing those critical real-time issues faced by the Nagchaw

Nation, I didn't see the full reality of our people being addressed. I now know that children exposed to violence often become victims of physical abuse too. This leaves them at risk for both physical and mental health disorders and the possibility of carrying on that violence in their intimate relationships as adults. As the Director of the Nagchaw Cultural Center I saw this to be an important Rez-wide initiative. An impactful decision that would affect the lives of our unborn relatives and reverberate throughout the next seven generations.

Violence against women and children was an issue that was very close to my heart. Having grown up as a child who witnessed domestic violence against my mother, I hated that my father was never held accountable. Before retiring to Flagstaff, Sam Gentry was a powerful member of the Coleman inner circle. Nobody dared to cross him given his explosive temper. As an adult that left me with my own set of intimacy issues. Thankfully, I began seeing a therapist during grad school. I know now that being exposed to domestic violence hurt my self-esteem and carried over into high school making it difficult for me to interact with boys; however, I was lucky having had an older brother who was nothing like my father. Keith served as a model for me in terms of understanding what a real man was like. Growing up with his "big brother" attention, and later the time he spent on our check-ins as we walked along the Snake River were vital to having survived my late childhood and adolescence.

Keeping his word, Stevie got my presentation onto the council's schedule three weeks from the day of our lunchtime discussion. On the day of the presentation Capt. Batton showed up, as well as Grandma Moon, Pawpaw, and Jericho Jefferson who represented the Elder's Council. At the last minute, Doc Watson, the Medical Director of the Native American Health Center also showed up, which certainly added more gravitas.

After my opening, Medical Social Worker Adriane Willis presented an anonymous case review from pediatrics and another from urgent care. Then I did an overview and my closing.

"Thank you, Adriane, the work you do at the health center is vital to the wellbeing of our people, and your support on this issue is necessary and appreciated.

"To recap what we've covered here today, nearly 55% of the women on Nagchaw have experience rape, physical violence, stalking, or psychological aggression in their lifetimes. Three quarters of those incidents have been at the hands of non-Native perpetrators, while a quarter have been Nagchaw intimate partners. All these women needed urgent or emergency care.

The invisible scars of domestic violence open the door to PTSD, self-medicating masked as increased alcohol and substance abuse, sleep disorders, chronic physical pain, severe depression, attempted and realized suicides. This vicious cycle, also known as intergenerational trauma, negatively impacts our families as exemplified by Adriane Willis' presentation. In the short term, we have a responsibility to begin doing everything we can to come into alignment with the reality of our people. In the long term, we need a plan that allows for healing the deep wounds that keep our people victims.

I know today's information hasn't been easy to listen to, but you showed up, and I thank you all for coming. I'll now open the floor for anything you might want to say at this time."

The room echoed a deafening silence, but after a brief period, a lively conversation ensued. The overwhelming consensus was that a Rez-wide campaign would be a start, and after that a designated team needed to begin assessing the local resources available for support services. Everyone present acknowledged that the short-term would be akin to a Band-Aid, but in the long term, the intergenerational trauma would begin being dealt with. After everyone left, Stevie came downstairs to my office and asked how I thought it went.

"Better than I imagined. Adrian's anonymous case reviews really got everyone's attention. How do you think it went?" I asked.

"The whole thing was impressive, Jos. Your

breakdown of the facts, the details of the anonymous case reviews, and your closing comments
were impactful. The serious conversation after
the presentation showed everyone how dire the
need is. Your Grandma Moon was a force too. I was
glad she shared that she's long carried the brunt
of this trauma in her role as Nagchaws Medicine
Woman. Her honesty about wanting more done
was forceful." Stevie said.

"Grandma has always been a force to be
reckoned with, just ask Pawpaw," I said as we
both laughed.

The next couple of months were intense, and
by Spring the campaign was ready to be launched.
I couldn't have done it without the support and
assistance of Adriane Willis, Lucy Keeton, and the
other council women; their help turned out to be
valuable beyond measure.

The Nagchaw Nation's annual Spring Fling
Crafts Festival was held every March around the
time of the Equinox. The Rez festival ground was
a large space with ample bleachers and was only
about a mile from the offices at Nagchaw Central.
There would be many visitors to the Rez for the
booths selling beautiful artwork, jewelry, leather
crafts, head scarves and hats, rugs, blankets,
handheld drums, and other beautiful, skillfully
made items. The Thunder Road Recovery men's
drumming group performed during the festival,

and it was good to see Mike Milton drumming along with them. In addition, there were food booths selling Indian tacos, fry bread, and other delectable edibles.

As an initial introduction Adriane, Lucy, and I had a domestic violence awareness booth under the banner of the Native American Health Center. In six months, we'll host a larger display at the fall Intertribal Powwow in October which was Domestic Violence Awareness month. For the Spring event, we had a special trifold brochure made with color pictures, as well as English on one side and the traditional River People dialect, or Uto-Aztecan language on the other.

"The DV brochure looks great! I think Coleman's Copy Central did a good job, don't you?" I asked.

"Yes, and all the freebees look good too. Purple representing domestic violence is a great choice since it also happens to be my favorite color." Adrian chuckled.

Our free giveaway items were all in purple: "Domestic Violence Awareness" ribbons, "Break the Silence" masks, "Domestic Violence Has No Place Here" bandanas, and #2 purple pencils that said, "Love Shouldn't Hurt" printed in gold, and of course, a large purple bowl of Bazooka bubble gum and miniature-candy bars. Although we were each wearing a stick and peel name badge, we put our business cards on the table should anyone want to contact us about the subject matter afterwards. As a team, we rotated our breaks so that there'd always be two of us at the table.

On my lunch break, I couldn't resist checking out the craft tables, especially the jewelry tables. At the encouragement of my beloved brother Keith, I had a table at the annual Nagchaw festival selling a variety of my handmade crafts. My most popular items were my mosaic squares and my windchimes. The larger mosaic squares could be hung as an art piece, and the smaller ones on the stove as a spoon holder or for a hot pot. The windchimes were ornate and sounded great in a gentle breeze. Mom, Grandma Moon, and Pawpaw always had one hanging on their front porch. They made great birthday gifts and stocking stuffers, and both were always my best sellers.

As I was leaving the craft tables, I ran into Stevie. He looked to be right out of the latest issue of GQ Casual in his fitted faded blue jeans, a fitted black tee shirt and his Teva leather sandals. He wore his usual watch with a brown leather band, but on his other wrist was something new. A brown braided leather band with a silver clasp attached to a little silver eagle feather. I also noticed that he smelled like Sandalwood which was one of my favorite essence oils. His thick, black, shoulder-length hair hung freely, which made him ever more captivating.

"Hey, Jos, how are you? Check out my new accessory. They're selling them at the leather craft table around the corner," Stevie said, holding up his right wrist to show me the braided leather band with the little attached silver eagle feather.

"Very nice. It's your style and looks good on you," I said.

"Thanks. So, how's the DV booth doing? Are you getting many visitors?"

"Yes, more than I originally thought. Several have asked general questions, but a couple have been more specific about their experiences. We made sure to listen and if they were interested, Adriane scheduled time to talk further. She has another Licensed Clinical Social Worker on staff at the health center who is taking appointments. Only two so far have wanted to talk further, which is fine. It's a start and women are coming to our table, so that's the important thing."

"That's fantastic, Jos. You're right, it's a good start and the beginning of real change happening. I'm so proud of your work on this," Stevie gushed. "Hey, how about doing dinner after the festival? Are you available? 'Ayuu 'mashxa.' (Let's eat.)

There it was the invite that I'd been okay without repeating. How could I put off this gorgeous man, because...why? What believable reason would I have to say "no", even on such short notice. Old habits are hard to break as my mind raced through excuses about having to pack up and get the booth items back to the office and put away when Stevie interrupted my thoughts.

"Jos, I can help you get your supplies packed up. In fact, we can put them in the back of the Camino, and we'll swing by the office and drop them off before we head out. What do you say?"

Well, I had absolutely no excuse to not take him up on his offer for dinner now. Besides, not accepting his offer would be rude, and I already knew that I'd be famished by the time that things wrapped up at the festival closing.

"Sure, that's sounds like a plan, but I'll warn you now. I skipped lunch so that I could scour the craft tables, so I'll be plenty hungry when this is all over."

"Okay, good. I've been wanting to check out Coleman's new Cattleman's Steakhouse. I hear their lounge is nice. It's probably going to be busy, so we can start there with a drink and check it out. How does that sound?" he asked with a twinkle in his eye.

CHAPTER 5

Only the Half-truth

"The characteristics of a personality, the qualities that make one personality different from another, cannot be appreciated without an understanding of the karma that created those characteristics. They cannot always be understood in terms of the history of the personality because they may reflect experiences that predate the personality, in some cases by centuries."

~ Gary Zukav, from *Seat of the Soul*

When we got to Cattleman's Steakhouse, there was going to be a 20-minute wait to get seated, so we went into the lounge. It was a very rustic, warm, and casual setting and with James Taylor's 'Everyday' playing overhead, I began loosening up before drinks were ordered. We took a seat at the rustic old bar, and the bartender approached. Lo and behold it was the gangly redhead with freckles who also waited tables at Matta's, Tim McGee.

"Hi Tim. I didn't know you worked here too," I said with surprise.

"Hey Jos. Yes, here too, and I'm on call as a backup at The Scarab. It takes some doing to make a decent living in the food service industry. So, what's your poison this evening?" Tim asked.

"She'll have an amaretto and pink grapefruit juice, and I'll have a Corona, please," Stevie said.

"Now, amaretto and pink grapefruit juice, that's a new one! How'd you come up with that?" Tim asked.

"Well, it's the perfect drink for this arid desert environment. Plus, the sweet and sour combo is delicious. You should try it, Tim," I said.

"Oh, I'll have to. It sounds good," Tim said.

As we sipped our drinks, I found myself looking forward to knowing more about Stevie's personal life. What I knew of him initially came through Keith as they both ran track in high school. I knew Keith liked Stevie and called him a "straight shooter". I knew he grew up on the Rez with his father who was Nagchaw, and his mother was non-indigenous. I didn't know that she'd passed away from asthma when Stevie was in middle school. I'd heard that she was very likable and many on the Rez admired her musical talents. She played the piano and was apparently very talented.

I only knew him on a business or professional level. Even at our occasional Naturally Native lunches our conversations were always about work. I could be wrong, but I sensed that he preferred it that way. That was until he asked me out to dinner at Matta's. Since then, things have shifted. I can't say how exactly, but I felt an energy shift. I sensed that he felt it too.

"So, Jos, you've been under the gun with the center's activities. How are you holding up?" Stevie asked.

"Listen, being under the gun, as you call it, is a good thing. The fast pace appeals to me, and I've started to think that I'm as achievement oriented as Keith used to be. In the past I was always laid-back, flexible, and patient, especially compared to my brother. As I'm getting older, I'm becoming more and more like him," I said. Stevie laughed.

"Well, I knew your brother, and he was achievement oriented, a sports competitor, but you know, he had a laid-back side too. In fact, after our track meets, we'd drink a cold one at the Snake River, under the tree he said you two always sat at."

"Oh really, that's something else I didn't know about Keith. Since his passing I've found out a few things that I didn't know. It's been surprising because I always thought I knew everything about my brother."

"Aww Jos, it's not possible to know everything about a person. I mean, we all have our secrets, don't we?" Stevie asked.

"Humm, I'm not sure. I'll have to ponder that and get back to you," I said as we both chuckled.

We were seated at a table in the rear of the restaurant. This table was slightly apart from the crowded main dining area and more private. Our dinner conversation had a more personal flavor and revolved around his life growing up on the Rez. He also spoke a lot about his mother, Lily, and how much she meant to him. He remembers her as soft spoken, gentle, and creative. He stated that once he finds a woman like that, he'll marry her. He also talked about how his father's clan rallied around them both when his mom passed away. He stated that he would never have made it through that exceptionally difficult time without the love and support of the rest of their clan. He also said that he never understood why his mother's family had disowned her for marrying his father. Their only response to Lily's death was the sympathy bouquet they sent for her burial.

Later, I spoke about growing up in Coleman and living with my parents. I stated that childhood for Keith and me was no walk in the park. I talked about being aware of how much my mom gave up to marry my father. I also mentioned how upsetting it was for me growing up with the way Sam treated Keith. Sam's frequent comment to Keith saying that he acted like a "damn Indian" made it difficult for me to forgive him since Keith's passing.

I even shocked myself by mentioning that in grad school I started seeing a family therapist, which helped me immensely. I talked about being raised in a household where domestic violence was a part of the family fabric. I stated that now

I understood more fully why I'd developed avoidance strategies with men. My relationship with Keith was the one glimmer of hope where relating to men was concerned. I told Stevie I knew that healing from this kind of trauma would be a life-long venture and that I would probably never marry because of that.

"Gosh, Jos, I'd think twice about that. Never marrying seems severe considering that you've worked with a therapist around your family issues, don't you think?" Stevie asked.

"Well, maybe, but I know that recovering from that kind of trauma won't happen overnight. And it will probably take a good long whi e for complete healing. Besides, I don't think most men are aware of this kind of thing. Finding a partner who is both self-aware and aware of the issues with my history might be asking a lot of Great Spirit," I said.

"I think Great Spirit is fully capable of finding someone able to understand and deal with your history. Just don't shut the door on what the future might hold," Stevie said.

Eventually, the waiter came to our table with the check. We had both been so engaged in our conversation that we were completely unaware that the kitchen had stopped serving and the restaurant staff had started getting ready to close.

The ride home was quiet. I sensed that we were both tired after a long day and a deep dive into our emotional pasts. Stevie asked if I'd like to listen to some music on the ride back to Nagchaw, and I said yes. He pulled out an instrumental CD called Ancient Echoes by Steve Halpern from The Tranquility Zone. The music was intensely relaxing with a combination of harp, keyboards, and soft chanting. He said that his mom introduced him to this kind of music. I thoroughly enjoyed The Tranquility Zone music and felt so relaxed that I almost fell asleep.

Once we got to my place, he got out and opened my door and walked me to the front entrance.

"Thank you for coming out to dinner with me tonight, Jos. I've enjoyed getting to know you better and I hope we can do it again at some point. I know it's a little tricky, since we work together, but if we're careful, I think we can manage that," Stevie said.

"Yes, I enjoyed this too. As for doing this again, I'd like that. It's just dinner after all," I said, knowing that was only a half-truth.

Unlike the first time we went to dinner, he took my hand and pulled me toward him for a hug. Neither of us moved to break the hug and it lasted for what seemed like a long time but was probably only a few seconds. I honestly thought my heart was going to leap out of my chest cavity it was pounding so hard. I prayed that he didn't feel it.

That night I had an interesting dream. I was in a plush green valley, sitting on the side of a small lake surrounded by sunshine, butterflies, and songbirds. A person with a bright aura walked up to me and extended their hand to help me up. When I stood up, this person handed me a glistening silver envelope and said, "Is this what you're looking for?" Then they turned and walked away.

I couldn't see who this person was as their aura was so bright. I couldn't tell if they were male or female, only that I was attracted to this individual. I opened the silver envelope, and before I could see what was inside, I woke up. Perplexed, I tried going back to sleep hoping that the dream would finish, and I would see what was inside the silver envelope. I also wanted to see the face of the one gifting me, but that didn't happen.

The next morning, I was greeted by my mom with fresh brewed coffee and her made from scratch Nagchaw morning buns. My favorite baked good was made of a delicious, puffed pastry and chocked full of savory goodness with a selection of her garden herbs, scrambled eggs, and chorizo.

"Kawitsh xwiiv xoti? (What smells good?)" I asked coming into the kitchen.

"Shiyii. (Good morning) How are you, my daughter? How did your booth do, and the dinner afterwards?"

"Oh gosh, Mom. As an introduction, the DV awareness booth did well. We had several women visit asking questions. A couple of them are going to meet later with Adriane. I really wish that you had something like this available when you needed it."

"Aww, thanks, but I don't think I would have taken advantage of such a thing, Jos. I was too intimidated by your father. And for the longest time I lived in a fantasy world believing that Sam would change. These women you're reaching out to don't know how lucky they are that you, Adriane, and Lucy are there to help them," Mom said as her eyes welled with tears.

"Well, you're safe now Ma. I will never regret putting my so-called father in his place and telling him that we were leaving. He's still mad at me and I can live with that." I said feeling the anger rising in my chest.

"You're going to have to forgive him at some point. You know that don't you?"

"Have you forgiven him, Mom?"

"No, but I'm working on it and sooner or later it will happen. I don't want to carry the burden of anger any longer than necessary. Going to Grandma's Medicine Circles has helped. Being with other women who understand and support me has allowed me to get a lot of bad medicine out of my system," Marta said and then paused and changed the subject. "So, how was Cattleman's Steakhouse? How was your dinner with Stevie Bahe?"

"Oh, Cattleman's is a nice restaurant. You and Jericho should check it out. The food was good and reasonably priced too. And our dinner conversation was, well, it was...interesting, is what I'd call it. Stevie told me about his childhood, and his mother, Lily. He loved her so much and still misses her."

"And did you talk about your childhood and family?"

"I did, a little. He was already aware of Sam's reputation, so nothing I said surprised him. Apparently, he and Keith were more than running buddies. They hung out now and again after track meets. Another Keith revelation, it seems."

"Aww, yes, your surprising brother! Do you think you'll go out with Stevie again?"

"Now, Ma. Since we work together, I'm not sure."

"May I be so bold to tell you, daughter, that I sincerely hope you do. Stevie Bahe is a wonderful young man. He'd be so good for you, Joslin."

"Yes, Mom, I know, but we've both got our priorities. He's not unlike Keith where it concerns the Rez. I mean, he's committed to bringing change that will benefit the Nagchaw Nation and sees that as his life's mission. Yep, he's very Keith-like, I'd say," I said. Truth be told, I had the same thought after the Cattleman's dinner. We're both committed to the work we're doing, so it's import-ant that nothing jeopardizes that. It was going to be a challenge, and I needed to tell Stevie to be careful around Lucy Keeton. She's mentioned his marital status to me a handful of times. Plus, I've heard through the Rez grapevine that she's someone who fancies herself as a matchmaker. I'll have to speak with her about that and nip this in the bud before the rumor mill gets wind of anything.

On Monday morning when Stevie came into the building and saw me, he smiled and said, "Good morning." I felt my stomach quiver.

"So, how are you?" he asked.

"Good, and you?" I parroted.

"Great, I really enjoyed our time together. Hey, let's do lunch this week. Let me know when you're available, okay?"

"Oh no, not this week? This week, and for the next couple, I'm going to be up to my neck finishing a couple of projects. Maybe later, I'll let you know when I'm available next, okay?"

"Really, well, okay. Sounds good. Have a good day," he said as he went upstairs to the council offices.

I hated that I gave him the cold shoulder, but after further contemplation, I was pretty sure going down this path wasn't going to be a good decision for me. After all, there were just too many pitfalls and I'd already been through enough to last a lifetime.

As I was heading into my office, I overheard the council's front desk receptionist, Rachel, directing someone downstairs to see me. As I looked up, I saw a striking man who looked to be

30-something and Nagchaw. He walked up and stuck out his hand.

"*Shiyii.* (Greetings.) My name is Klay; I'm the son of Mary Swiftwater. I was wondering if we could schedule an appointment to talk about a potential project, I'd like to have the Nagchaw Cultural Center co-sponsor?" he asked.

"I'm Joslin Gentry, the Director of the Nagchaw Cultural Center. "Come on into my office and let's talk about your project," I said.

I took a seat at my desk, and he sat across from me in one of two available chairs. Klay stood about 5'11' with a once traditional cut. His black hair was growing out, which gave him a shaggy appearance. He wore Levi's, a blue workman's shirt with the sleeves rolled up to his elbows, and a worn pair of Reebok's. He also had a water bottle carrier strapped across his chest. He reached for it and took a drink.

"Yes, since moving back from Flagstaff, snow country, I'm parched most of the time. I'd forgotten how dry and hot it is here," Klay said.

"I understand. The Flagstaff environment is much different than the desert. So, tell me, Mr. Swiftwater, what's on your mind."

"Thank you for seeing me without an appointment, and please, call me Klay. I really didn't expect that we'd be speaking today; however, I'll take this opportunity to talk with you about two things I love, science and teaching."

"Those are two things certainly worth loving," I said.

"Yes, they are. Prior to moving back to Nagchaw I was a college prep teacher at Flagstaff High School. I love science, more specifically physics, and earth science. I believe that First Nations children need opportunities to see and understand how it is that the teachings of the Nagchaw Ancients and science are two sides of one coin, so to speak.

"I know having taught in a public school system that nobody is looking out for our Indigenous children. There are no programs exposing them to the interesting things they could learn about science and math. I'd like to create a program for Nagchaw grade school aged kids that offers them the chance to be exposed to math and science in such a way that it taps into their cultural creativity. The overall goal would be to ignite a flame that allows them to continue with their high school and then post high school education.

"I have lots of ideas that I've used in the college prep classroom, but they can be adjusted for lower grade levels. I'd like to do this on a part-time basis to start while I'm here looking after my Nthay (mother). "

"Gosh, Klay, that's a fantastic idea. Why don't you write up a proposal laying out your intention, objectives, the curriculum, and the length of the program, as well as a projected budget. Be sure to include any other details that would clarify what it is you'd like to do. I'll present it to the Tribal Council, and we can talk after that. How does that sound?"

"Great! I've already got a rough draft. I'll finish that up, do a budget, and have it to you in the next few days. Thank you so much for your time, Ms. Gentry," he said glancing at his watch. "I must leave now. I have an appointment with the health center social worker to talk about my mother."

"How is she doing? I know it's been difficult for her since your father passed."

"She's struggling, but I believe what she's going through is her grieving process. Unfortunately, she's convinced that she's dying. I spoke with Doc Watson who said that's not so. I need someone to give me some advice about how to deal with this. Doc Watson put me in touch with Adriane Willis, which I hope will help."

"Oh, yes, grief really does feel like death. I've been there and it takes a while to get past that stage. I know your being back will help with her healing process. And Adriane will be helpful too, I'm sure. You know, I can mention her to my grandma. I know they know each other, and it might be helpful for her," I said.

"If you're talking about Medicine Woman Grandma Moon, then yes, I know she respects her and would love to hear from her. Please mention my mother to her, and I'll be in touch. Thanks again," he said as he left the office.

CHAPTER 6

As Different as We Are Alike...

"Anything that increases separation within a person shatters the soul or in some form diminishes its strength, is not to be confused with its immortality. The soul, as it reduces itself to fit into a physical incarnation, has the blueprint of holism in it. A genetic spiritual pattern, so to speak, of holism is there and present, and when the personality operates outside of the genetic pattern of holism, dysfunction results."

~ Gary Zukav, from *Seat of the Soul*

There was an interesting alignment of personalities in my family. Me, Mom, and Pawpaw were the family introverts while Grandma Moon, Keith, Sam, and Jericho were the extroverts. Although I had become more outgoing since Keith's passing, I knew that at my core I was still an introvert. I was comfortable being alone, uncomfortable in large groups, did not like being the center of attention, and given a choice would prefer a small circle of close friends. On the other hand, Keith, rest his soul, had always been quick to develop relationships, preferred being around people, was not a fan of routine, and thrived being the center of attention. I speak of this contrast of personalities only to say that as a family we were as different as we were alike.

Looking from the outside, the reunion of Marta Yellowbird and Jericho Jefferson was viewed by those of the Nagchaw Nation as inevitable and long overdue. Looking from my perspective, with an understanding of her history, I know that my mother sacrificed and suffered because of the choices she made decades ago. She married a man who did not respect her or her son. She denied Jericho the opportunity to raise his son, and for that Jericho had to forgive her. The coldness and brutality with which she lived for so long shattered her spirit. My mother was aware that she needed to heal from the long-term toxicity. It was as if she'd fed herself poison for a long time.

My mother sought council and healing from Grandma Moon, not as her mother but the Nagchaw Medicine Woman. As for Jericho, he and Mike Milton had been spending time together in deep conversation. My hunch was that they were seeking council from each other about the loss of a beloved son and a best friend. Additionally, Jericho had forgiven my mother. He wanted a fresh start, which they were both working toward.

It's been my experience that healing takes its own sweet time. First, both my mother and Jericho were grieving for the loss of their son. He was also grieving the loss of all the years that he could have been involved with Keith but wasn't. I knew that was a hard one to let go of, even for a compassionate man like Jericho Jefferson. Still, they loved each other. They were working toward healing and moving forward. Often in life, this is what it all boils down to and it is a blessing when it happens. I would be lucky to have someone in my life who felt that deeply about me and would be willing to love me, flaws and all.

"It's going to take time to heal from your father's abuse over all those years, but I'm working on it. I'm so grateful to have Jericho back in my life. I should never have left him, and I paid a heavy price for that mistake," Mom said.

"Jericho still seems to have deep feelings for you, Mom. I know Keith cared for him too. What an unexpected twist to a tragic story. Sometimes I cannot believe what we've all been through and survived," I said.

"I know, some days all I can do is shake my head. I have considered the possibility that Jericho could have held what I did against me. Denying him a relationship with his son, but instead, he's forgiven me."

"Mom, I know that Keith would be pleased about how things have turned out. With you and Jericho, with me, and with Stevie as the Tribal Council Chief Executive. Of everyone who might have filled that seat, I know Stevie is the one Keith would have most approved of."

"And about what is developing between you and Stevie?" Mom asked.

"Mom, please, beyond coworkers and friends, there is nothing else happening between Stevie and me."

I wasn't completely honest; however, I wasn't yet ready to be anything more than coworkers and friends with Stevie Bahe. I had too much to do, and the distraction of his presence was more than I could manage on top of everything else.

Later that week, Klay Swiftwater stopped by the office to drop off his proposal for the youth workshop. He mentioned his visit with Medical Social Worker, Adriane Willis, and said that his mother was asking for a Healing Circle.

"Good morning Ms. Gentry, do you have a minute to talk?" Klay said.

"Sure Klay, come in, how's you mother doing?" I asked.

"Somewhat better, but what's changed the most is my understanding and ability to deal with her. I was aware that how she was feeling was due to her grieving process, but my difficulty was the way in which she was expressing herself. It really bothered me that she was talking as if she would be dying soon too. I know that is a pattern that often happens with couples who've been married for a long time, so it worried me. Adriane had some insight I hadn't considered. She also had some helpful tips, and she came out to the house to see mom, which really helped," Klay said.

"Oh good, I was sure that Adriane would be helpful. She's a valuable resource for the Nagchaw Nation, for sure. We are so lucky to have a medical social worker who is Nagchaw and lives as one of us," I said.

"So, Ms. Gentry, my mother and Grandma Moon had discussed holding a Healing Circle when she came to visit. Can you tell me how to get a hold of Grandma Moon?" Klay asked.

"Oh, sure. Your mother can call her, let me give you her phone number," I said.

"Yes, we have her phone number, but my mother won't call her. She believes her spirit is weak, and if she speaks on the phone, it will drain her vital energy. I've tried to explain to her that that's not true, but she simply won't believe me. I thought it best if I went by to speak with Grandma Moon myself," Klay said.

I told Klay where our place was and that if he went now, he'd be able to catch her outside tending to her garden. He seemed appreciative and then his next question surprised me even more.

"You've been more than helpful Ms. Gentry. As a gesture of my appreciation, I'd like to take you to lunch sometime. I hear Naturally Native has great Indian tacos," Klay said.

"Oh, thank you, but that's not necessary. I'm happy to assist you with anything that will help your mother get through such a difficult time. Grieving the loss of someone we love is more than tragic. It's a whirlwind that shakes many things loose and causes us to become disoriented. Getting through something like that is import-ant. The sun will rise when the brown eagle soars again," I said.

"Awe, yes, the brown eagle lore. I've not heard any mention of that since I've been back, but I know my mother is steeped in that tradition. Signs are always something she's paid attention to. If I may, I'll use your statement with her. It's poetic and she'll love it."

"Of course, if it helps use it. On second thought, Klay, let's go to lunch. I'm due for one of their tasty Indian tacos."

"Great, how's Thursday?" Klay asked.

"Thursday's good," I said.

"What time do you normally go to lunch? I'll stop here and we can walk over," Klay said.

"How's 1:30 pm?"

"Great. I'll see you on Thursday," Klay said as he turned and left the office.

What in the world was I thinking, was my first thought after Klay left. It was so unlike me to impulsively change my mind like that. My brother used to say that sometimes making an impulsive decision is a little push from the spirit world in a direction we might not have aptly considered. I guess I'll find out at lunch on Thursday.

The next morning shortly after I'd arrived the Tribal Council office manager, Allie, came down to my office. She had come in early before everyone else came in.

"Good morning, Joslin, I wanted to speak with you before the rest of the gang rolled in, if you've got a few minutes," Allie said.

"Sure Allie, what's going on? I can't remember ever seeing you here this early, except maybe before the Spring Fling Festival," I said.

"I know, but I really wanted to speak with you privately. Something out of the ordinary happened yesterday with Klay Swiftwater. Before he came by to meet you, he stopped in and came upstairs. He saw me and asked to speak with me, so we went into my office. Then he started asking me about your job. How long you'd been in the position, was it a position requiring an election like the council seats, and did I know if you had plans to leave the position anytime soon. Honestly, Joslin, he kind of freaked me out with all those questions. Then, before he left, he asked that I not mention his questions to you," Allie said.

"Whoa, now that's interesting. I wonder why he just didn't ask me when he came in to see me? Well, he's invited me out to lunch tomorrow, so

I'll feel him out and see if I can figure out what's going on," I said.

"And don't worry Allie, I won't mention that we spoke," I said.

After learning about Klay's questioning of our office manager, Allie, I pondered the real reason he invited me to lunch. I wrestled with this well into the night until I was finally able to fall asleep. Upon waking, I recalled a brief dream sequence which had me questioning Klay Swiftwater's intentions even more.

As I walk toward an open doorway, I see Klay sitting behind a large desk in a shadowy office. He is wearing a black Armani suit with a burgundy shirt and a black tie. He invites me to come in and take a seat across from him. The chair he motions for me to sit in is a child's red plastic folding chair. Then he shoves a sheet of paper in front of me and asks me to sign it. Just as I start to ask if there's another chair I can sit in, I wake up.

I won't stir the pot. I will avoid creating conflict and be careful not to disrupt the status quo in answering his questions about my role as the Director of the Nagchaw Cultural Center. If his intentions are anything other than enjoying lunch together, I'll do my best to root out what exactly he's contemplating.

CHAPTER 7

Challenging Old Patterns

"The center of the evolutionary process is choice. It is the engine of our evolution. Each choice that you make is a choice of intention. You may choose to remain silent in a particular situation, for example, and that action may serve the intention of penalizing, sharing, compassion, extracting vengeance, showing patience, or loving. You may choose to speak forcefully, and that action may serve any of the same intentions. What you choose, with each action and each thought, is an intention, a quality of consciousness that you bring to your action or your thought."

~ Gary Zukav, from *Seat of the Soul*

That morning as I got dressed, I found myself feeling self-conscious about holding the director's position. All those old feelings of inadequacy were surfacing again. Honestly, I thought I'd worked through all that. How is it that simply hearing about Klay's inquiry about my position now finds me feeling insecure? After all this time, I'm still dealing with those tired old feelings! I threw my hairbrush across my bedroom, hitting the wall and scaring my tabby cat, Luna, napping on my bed.

"Gee thanks, Dad! Because of your lack of encouragement for my entire life, I'm still dealing with this shit! Why didn't you see fit to give even the tiniest bit of emotional support to Keith and me?" I said out loud as I finished getting dressed and headed out the door.

Klay came to my office at 1:30 pm. From there, we walked three blocks to the Naturally Native Café and ordered our lunch. He was in good spirits and spoke openly about his prior position in the college preparatory program at Flagstaff High School.

"You sound like you really miss the work you were doing and your students," I said.

"I do. It was challenging and fulfilling. It won't be easy to find something like that again," Klay said.

"Oh, you never know, Klay. Coleman High might need an experienced teacher who's run a college preparatory program."

"Perhaps, but I don't have much faith in the traditional educational system for accurately evaluating and addressing deficits. I believe that they are blind when it comes to understanding the needs of our Indigenous children," Klay said.

"So, if not in a traditional school system, where do you see yourself finding the kind of work you'd like to do?" I asked.

"Well, to be honest, I'd love to have a position like yours. I would be a good fit for the kind of work you're doing."

I was surprised by his directness and found myself unsure of how to address his remark.

"Oh, with your experience and educational background I'm sure you'd be great in the director's position. Having grown up as Nagchaw, you're ready made for this kind of work," I said.

"Yes, I had heard about the position through my mother and intended to apply. I was thinking about submitting my application now and asking them to keep it on file in case you decide to leave," Klay said.

"Well, Klay, you could do that, but I have no plans on leaving anytime soon. My 5-year plan has me here in this position," I said.

"Good to know. Maybe I'll wait a while and see if my youth program is approved. That would certainly put a feather in my cap and might help me get into the position at some later date."

This conversation left me more than a little peeved and wanting to say, *'Kadok m'iim'?!* (What did you say?!) After all, the nerve of this man to come right out and tell me he wants my job while I'm still in the position. Oh, how I wished Keith were still around. He'd know exactly how to handle Klay's remarks.

Our remaining lunchtime conversation was sparse as I wasn't in the mood for chatting. He sensed that he'd crossed the line. He was not very talkative, which was fine with me.

After lunch we walked back to the Tribal Council offices and said our goodbyes. As I entered the building, Stevie was coming downstairs motioning that he wanted to see me.

"Hey Joslin, do you have a minute to talk?" Stevie asked.

"Sure, let's go into my office," I said.

"So, I heard you went to lunch with Klay Swiftwater. How'd that go?" Stevie asked.

"Not well at all," I said.

"No? What happened?" Stevie asked.

"Oh, not much...other than the fact that he admitted to wanting my job," I said.

"No, he didn't! Allie told me about the questions he was asking her the other day. And I wanted to ask you about his youth program proposal. It's a good idea and I don't think it will take much to sell it to the council," Stevie said.

"Well good, then. I'll just have to get used to having someone around who is waiting for me to leave so he can take over my job," I said.

"Well, that's actually what I wanted to talk to you about," Stevie said.

Suddenly my heart began to palpitate as I heard what Stevie was saying. Did he want Klay Swiftwater to take over my job? My stomach began to churn as I remembered my dream. Was that what the dream with Klay behind a desk was about? What on earth was going on? I felt as if I'd walked into a nightmare. I felt as if I was going to be sick, was Stevie going to give my job to Klay?

"Okay, Joslin, here's the situation. One of the council members is considering resigning for personal reasons. Normally, that would require an election allowing others on the Rez to run a campaign and then there'd be an election. Unless, of course, there was someone already on staff who met the criteria and wanted to transition into that seat," Stevie said.

"Are you asking me if I'd like to transition to a Tribal Council seat?" I asked.

"Well, this person hasn't officially said anything yet, but it's been mentioned to me that his resignation is coming. So, when that seat opens, then yes," Stevie said.

"Oh gosh, that's a relief. I thought you were going to tell me that you felt Klay Swiftwater would be better suited for my job," I said.

"Well, he could certainly do the job, but I'm not sure if he's better suited for the position, Jos. I just wanted to see if you had any interest in becoming a council member," Stevie said.

"I feel that the Cultural Center's mission and programming are very much aligned with my interests and abilities. I don't think I'd make a very good politician," I said.

"Well, you could learn to be, but you'd have to have an interest in being more political, which sounds like you are not up for doing," Stevie said.

"I'm not interested in doing that kind of work. It requires a wide range of skills, viewpoints, and experience from one's background, which I really don't have," I said.

"You know, Jos, a large part of the job requires building partnerships, seeking resources, and speaking with Tribal members which you have done, so don't sell yourself so short. You just don't have a desire to be on the Tribal Council if I'm hearing you correctly," Stevie said.

"Yes, that's right. That might change some day, but probably not anytime soon," I said.

"Okay then, that's what I wanted to check out with you. As for Klay Swiftwater, his proposal looks good, and I'm sure that the council will approve it and his budget. Don't let this overly ambitious guy scare you Jos, you're in the director's position and doing a great job. Like I said, I haven't met him yet, but Allie thinks Klay's one of those overly ambitious, intellectual types who apparently lacks social skills," Stevie said.

Stevie left my office as the front desk receptionist, Rachel, called downstairs to say that there was someone who wanted to speak with him. I couldn't help but feel that Stevie was somewhat disappointed that I had no interest in transitioning onto the Tribal Council.

Could it be that he would like to have more direct contact with me, or that he thinks I'd be a good Tribal Advocate, or maybe both?

The following week, the council met, discussed, and asked me about the cultural value of Klay's proposal, and then convened to vote. After a brief time, I was informed that the council had unanimously approved of Klay's program with one caveat. I was directed to oversee his work while allowing him as much leeway as he needed in structuring his workshop, which I was happy to do. After all, Klay is a math and science nerd.

Klay was elated about his proposal being approved and said that he'd start talking up the workshop around Nagchaw. He said he'd like it covered in the Tribal Voice and asked me about doing that.

"I'm wondering if doing a piece in the monthly edition of the Tribal Voice about the workshop would help. Sort of a general outline and letting parents and youth know how to sign up," Klay said.

"Good idea, let me call Tribal Voice and speak with the editor Jackie Rivers about doing that. She'll want to run a "Special Edition," which would be an introduction piece about you and your background, as well as a couple of pictures, the workshop overview, and the how-to for signing up," I said.

"Do you have a timeline for starting?" I asked.

"Well, for the first run in two months as a summer series, and if that goes well, one in the fall and then again in the spring, for three times a year. The workshops will increase in their subject matter once the group has absorbed the material. I say absorbed because this will be a grade-free-zone which I have found most kids welcome. No worries about failing, just being curious, asking questions, making observations, and doing simple experiments. There won't be any limit to how often kids can enroll. They can sign up as often as they'd like," Klay said.

"Okay, great, I've got that on my list of calls to make for today. I know she'll want to interview you, so look for a call from her. Keep me posted, and we can meet later to schedule a firm start time before your interview," I said.

Later that evening while cleaning up the kitchen after Mom and I finished eating, my mind started wandering. I began thinking about the possibility of moving into that Tribal Council seat and Klay Swiftwater taking over my position in the Cultural Center. I still can't see myself as a council member, but who knows, maybe someday. I'm halfway through my current five-year plan, so I don't see any changes coming soon, but who knows. As I am aware, life sometimes works out differently than you expect it to.

The next morning, I had a couple of stops to make before going into the office, but once I got in Rachel called downstairs saying that Mr. Bahe wanted to speak with me. She reiterated that he wanted to speak with me as soon as I came in, so I put my things down and went upstairs immediately.

"Good morning, Stevie. How are you?" I asked.

"Concerned Jos, please come in and sit down," Stevie said.

"I want you to know that I'm more shocked and confused by what I'm about to tell you. So, this morning, I was greeted with a petition signed by 65 tribal members asking that you be replaced, and Klay Swiftwater be assigned to your director's position," Stevie said.

"What? You've got to be kidding, Stevie," I said.

"Jos, I wish I were. Even though 65 is a small percentage of the tribal members, still, I'm just shocked. Why would Mr. Swiftwater do this just as his program has been approved? It makes no sense to me. Jos, did something happen between you two that you haven't told me about?" Stevie asked.

"No, Stevie, nothing other than what I'd mentioned about him making it very clear that he wanted my job. I tried to appear not threatened. I even stated that I thought he'd make a good director, but that I had no plans to leave the position anytime soon," I said.

I sat in Stevie's office stunned and unable to collect myself. Slowly, I felt the pressure rising in my chest as my eyes began to well with tears. Then, I felt a strong 'no way' reverberate in my chest. I was not going to crumble under this challenge. As soon as I had that thought, I heard

Keith's voice...

> *"Sister, you are enough. You can face anyone who yearns for what is yours. Know that their yearning comes from a hallow space and those who appear to be a threat, are moving from a place of weakness. You face no threat."*

The fact that Klay took the time and energy to collect signatures meant that he sought tribal members out, and that was a real concern. Not to mention that I hated that it drudged up all my old insecurities about being inadequate and not good enough.

"So, Jos, I checked the security camera, and Klay dropped the envelope addressed to me in the mail slot early this morning before any of us came in, so let me speak with him first."

"Fine with me, I don't think I can speak with him about it today anyway. I'm too upset and will probably say something I'll regret, which won't help," I said.

"No, you don't have to see or speak with him today. I'll deal with him and let you know how that goes. I can't believe that he would do something like this. I've heard that he's an intelligent guy, so it's surprising that he would do something so inconsiderate and presumptuous," Stevie said.

It was more than surprising to me; it was downright insulting. It was as if I was incapable of doing the job and he just decided that he'd be better suited for the position. How dare he come back to Nagchaw Nation and try to slither his way into my job. A position I earned outright and have put my heart and soul into.

As promised, Stevie met with Klay and addressed the petition and his motivation for taking on the task of getting signatures as well as the timing. I didn't sleep well that entire week and knew that I also needed to address this incident with him before we met to discuss his starting schedule. I called Klay and asked him to come into the office to discuss his petition, which he immediately started apologizing for over the phone. I cut him off and told him to wait until we could meet face to face.

I knew from what Stevie said that he went at him hard and stated that his actions were inexcusable. By submitting the petition Klay managed to put a black mark against his ever being seriously considered for the director's position for mishandling this situation. Still, I wanted to stress how his actions affected me personally and would go at him on a level that he's most uncomfortable and unfamiliar with, my feelings.

Klay arrived on time as he entered my office with an uneasy gait and took a seat. I decided to skip the formal niceties and jump right in.

"I cannot tell you how hurtful your petition was. I thought I made it clear that I wasn't going anywhere, and yet, you decided trying to oust me was worth your time and energy. Did you not believe me when I stated I had no plans to go anywhere anytime soon?" I asked.

Klay sat staring down at the floor for a good while before answering me. Looking at him I saw a little boy who seemed out of place and was not a part of his surroundings. Even though that might be his underlying motivation, which he might not be fully aware of, I wanted to make my position felt.

"No, I heard you, and I'm so sorry. I also heard you say that I'd make a great director and was ready-made for the position. Then I heard that you were moving to an open Tribal Council seat, and I thought this would be the time to be preemptive," Klay said.

"What? I'm not moving to the council; although I was asked if I was interested. Who in the world told you that?" I asked.

"Oh, well, it was just some scuttlebutt I accidentally overheard at Naturally Native, so the petition was intended to give me the edge," Klay said.

"Klay, why didn't you just come to me to verify if what you heard was accurate? I would have gladly told you that it was not going to happen," I said.

"Well, I guess I wanted it to be true, so I just bought into the rumor, which was really stupid," Klay said.

"Yes, it was stupid Klay, and you're not a stupid person, so that's why it was so surprising to Mr. Bahe and shocking to me. You've done some damage to your reputation with that poorly timed decision; however, hopefully, with enough time devoted to your youth workshop series people will forgive and forget," I said.

"But will you forgive and forget?" Klay asked.

I took a little longer than usual pause for this answer.

"Well, it's said that time heals all wounds. I'm sure if you devote yourself to your youth workshop series like I believe you will, we will get through this unfortunate mishap," I said.

Klay and I finished our conversation and ended with scheduling the start of his workshop series "Exploring the Ancients Universe and Beyond". After Klay left, before I could pick up the phone to intercom Stevie, he was standing in my office doorway.

"Well, I didn't hear any screaming so I'm guessing your meeting with Klay went well?" Stevie said.

"Yes, better than I expected," I said.

"Did he tell you why he thought the petition was a good idea?" Stevie asked.

"Yes he did, and it's hard to believe that a rumor of my taking a council seat is already out there," I said.

"Well, I received Ernie Klinton's resignation last week," Stevie said.

"If only Klay would have come to me to check out the validity of the rumor, we could've skipped this mess," I said.

"True, but I believe it's clearer to him now that

you're committed to YOUR job. Klay's just going to have to wait until that changes before he'll get a crack at it," Stevie said.

"Yes, I believe you're right. Hey, I'm starving, let's finish this conversation and go to lunch," I said.

"Okay, sounds good, Stevie said.

Our walk to Naturally Native was energized and delightful. It had been a while since we'd been to lunch, and I could tell Stevie missed our time together. Truth be told, so did I.

The lunchtime waitress, Emmy, greeted us and then seated us in the back before bringing our menus and water. Always the bubbly personality, Em seemed more so than usual today which led to my inquiry.

"So, what's happening with you Emmy?" I asked.

"Wow, haven't you guys heard?" Emmy asked.

"No, what are you talking about?" Stevie asked.

"So, there's this very powerful Medicine Man who used to be a part of Nagchaw, and he's back now, and holding sessions with anyone who wants to meet with him," Emmy stated.

"What kind of sessions?" Stevie asked.

"What's his name?" I asked.

"He's holding visioning sessions; you know, where he tells you what your future will be. Although I never heard of him, I know several older tribal members have, and his name is

Jason Blackrock," Emmy said.

Stevie and I looked at each other in shock. Jason Blackrock was a name neither of us ever expected to hear again.

"He's charging, but not much, so I'm saving my tip money, because I want to do a session with him," Emmy said.

CHAPTER 8

The Prodigal Son

"Each soul comes to the Earth with gifts. A soul does not incarnate only to heal and to balance its energy, to pay its karmic debts, but also to contribute its specialness in specific ways. Each soul brings the particular configuration of the Life force that it is to the needs of the Earth school. It does this with purpose and intention."

~ Gary Zukav, from *Seat of the Soul*

Years earlier, before Keith and I were born, the Nagchaw Nation proudly touted the wisdom, visions, and healing abilities of one of its own, a highly revered young Nagchaw Medicine Man named Jason Blackrock. Grandma Moon spoke to me about Jason at length since I became her mentee.

Early on, I never clearly understood the depth of her spiritual sight, but as time went on that changed. I was always careful about following her direction because I understood that Grandma Moon can see things not apparent to myself or others. And Jason Blackrock's story is a prime example.

The Blackrock clan had longstanding indigenous roots in the desert southwest. Jason came to the forefront by way of his dreams and visions, which guided the Nagchaw Nation toward prosperity in the earliest days. His acclaim was widespread, and well known amongst the tribes throughout the desert southwest until the day he disappeared.

Born of Indigenous parents, Jason came from a long line of Medicine Men, so it was no surprise when he started showing signs of being a spiritually gifted adolescent. His mother, ShuShu Blackrock, reached out to Grandma Moon asking her to mentor Jason because his father and grandfather were now deceased. Grandma Moon accepted the task and took Jason on as her mentee until he reached the age of 20. During that time, Jason flourished and matured as a young Medicine Man. Many believed that he was more gifted than either his father or grandfather had been.

In the beginning, Jason's sessions provided spiritual guidance and a path toward healing as an extension of the person's everyday life. He communicated with spirit guides, the Nagchaw Ancestors, and he worked with dreams as a vehicle for progressing on one's spiritual journey. Known to be able to bend time and space, Jason could project alternative futures, by way of the dreams, of those who came to him. He was known to astral travel for the benefit of assisting those who were in danger of being possessed by demonic forces, or to see the future, or to support healing the sick. Jason Blackrock was on his way to being a very gifted Medicine Man.

At 20, Grandma Moon did not think he was ready to go out on his own, but Jason insisted. Grandma Moon's doubts about his readiness were because she knew there had been some kind of past life trauma that would disrupt his development if not dealt with. She urged him to do a soul retrieval which would take him into the Spirit World to identify and heal this past life trauma. A soul retrieval would have further stabilized Jason spiritually and psychologically, but he adamantly insisted that he didn't need to do this kind of work on himself.

His legacy came crashing down when he took leave without anyone knowing why he left or where he went. Jason had not been heard from for over two years. Upon his return his appearance had drastically changed. He was disheveled and smelled of alcohol and no longer was interested in working with his spiritual gifts. In the weeks since he'd returned, he'd said very little about where he'd been or why he chose to leave without making his whereabouts known.

Upon Jason's return his mother ShuShu Blackrock reached out to Grandma Moon asking her to come to her home and see Jason. He confessed to Grandma Moon that he'd crossed into the spirit world and experienced a horrific atrocity that occurred in a recent past life. Yes, this was the traumatic event that Grandma Moon felt he needed to heal by way of a soul retrieval. It was clear that this unresolved trauma was why he had left without saying anything to anyone.

"Tell me Jason, why did you not come to me? If you would have come to me, I would have helped you." Grandma Moon said.

"I couldn't come to you. You told me that I wasn't ready to go out on my own. I arrogantly dismissed your warning and refused to do a soul retrieval. Then I witnessed the horrific event that you knew would traumatize me. I couldn't believe that the bloodbath from that atrocity had happened to me. Bringing that into my consciousness, I will never be able to return to doing the kind of spiritual work that I had been doing. I've been destroyed, ruined and it's my own fault," Jason said with tears streaming down his cheeks.

"Yes, you have suffered, then and now, but your gifts have not left you. You are still capable of working for the betterment of others who need your help. Jason, you can use what's happened to deepen your understanding, and abilities, but you must deal with the trauma and not run from it. Running from our pain and sorrow only gives our suffering more power."

"I don't know if I'm able to deal with what I saw and experienced. It was beyond anything I have ever thought about or witnessed. It was like I was there and experiencing torture again, for the first time. I cannot, I will not go through that again."

"That is your decision, but you need to think about why it is that you are choosing to turn your back on your gifts. What if Great Spirit showed you what happened so that you could progress past that trauma and come out on the other side stronger and more resolute? Jason, you have spirit helpers. Our ancestors, the Nagchaw Ancients, surround you now as they did before you were shown this traumatic event. They are here because you are connected to them, and their assistance is available if you ask. Have you considered that?"

Grandma Moon got up and moved closer to sit next to Jason. She took his hand and they both sat in silence. Then she got up and poured Jason a cup of her cleansing tea and handed it to him.

"Drink this remedy of Chamomile, Morning Glory, and Sweetgrass. These herbs were grown in my garden. They will help clear your mind of anxiety and allow you to sleep peacefully while preventing nightmares. It will open your heart to see what road you should travel, to come back into alignment with Mother Earth and the four directions."

"Thank you, Grandma, you have given me much to pray about. I will consider all that you have said. We will speak again soon. I am so tired; I must sleep now. Thank you again for coming to see me."

Five days passed before Jason contacted Grandma Moon. After wrestling with what she had said to him, he knew he needed a cleansing detox and decided to do the soul retrieval. Jason understood that taking this action would help resolve what he'd experienced during his vision of that past life trauma.

The night before the spiritual intervention, Grandma Moon gave Jason these instructions and handed him a small container of oil.

"Eat a small evening meal of fresh fruit and vegetables. Before going to sleep, bathe, and then use this Angelica root and Sandalwood oil on your body. It has strong calming properties. It will allow you to sleep soundly and balance your emotions. It will also reduce any anxiety you might have about the next morning's ceremony. Then meet me at the Medicine Hogan at sunrise."

As the first hint of sunlight peeked over the horizon, a mild breeze blew through the desert as Jason walked to the Medicine Hogan where Grandma Moon and Pawpaw met him. They greeted Jason, and Grandma offered him a special blend of tea saying that it would allow the clearing and cleansing of anything harmful or negative. As Grandma smudged Jason with the smoke of Sage, she chanted a prayer calling on Great Spirit to restore his physical, emotional, and spiritual wellbeing, so that he could live in harmony with the environment and continue to walk the Red Road.

Outside the hogan, the Fire Keeper, Mike Milton, took heated rocks into the hogan's fire pit. The Thunder Road group began drumming as Jason removed his tee shirt and went inside bare chested and in shorts. Jason followed Grandma Moon and Pawpaw inside and lay on a woven grass mat. Grandma and Pawpaw prayed, chanted, and used a shamanic rattle over Jason calling on his spirit guides to assist him on his journey.

What I'm telling you about Jason Blackrock happened more than a decade before I became Grandma Moon's mentee. At first Jason seemed rescued by that spiritual intervention, but Grandma Moon stated that he never seemed quite right after the soul retrieval.

Jason's past life traumatic event happened in the late 1800's as one of the thousands of Indigenous children taken away from their families and tribes and forced to attend boarding schools. The goal was to have indigenous children assimilate into mainstream Euro-American culture. Upon entry to the schools these children were bathed in kerosene and forced to wear military-like uniforms. The boys' heads were shaved, and the girl's hair was cut short. They were given Anglo names and forbidden to speak their Native languages. These children were beaten severely when they did. There were frequent beatings, and many children did not survive. Jason's traumatic past life memory was as a child who was beaten beyond recognition and buried on the boarding school grounds.

Six months later, Jason Blackrock went missing again. The last time anyone heard from him he'd reportedly decided to travel another road. Those who knew Jason claimed that he moved to Sierra Vista and was drinking heavily. In addition, he was now considered to be a "plastic" medicine man, who was charging exorbitant prices for theatrical ceremonies for the non-indigenous tourist population. Pawpaw and Grandma Moon traveled to Sierra Vista to see Jason, but he refused to see them. Little did Jason know then that he'd be seeing them again a decade and a half later.

This experience broke Grandma's heart, but we all have the capacity to move between the light and the dark. Our decisions are our decisions, as they should be. Grandma especially understood as she and Pawpaw had both been boarding school children. She waits for Jason to return and believes that he will come home someday. To this day, Grandma Moon and Pawpaw remember Jason Blackrock in their daily prayers.

CHAPTER 9

Unfinished Business at Home

"When a soul incarnates, its memory of the agreement that it has made with the Universe becomes soft. It becomes dormant, awaiting the experiences that will activate it. These experiences are not necessarily experiences that the personality would choose. They are nonetheless necessary to the activation of the awareness of the power and the mission of the soul within the consciousness of the personality, and to its preparation for that task."

~ Gary Zukav, from *Seat of the Soul*

I t was the first of the month's council meeting. After a lively round of discussion about Klay Swiftwater's petition and the start of his *Exploring the Ancients Universe and Beyond* workshop, the council was anxious to discuss Jason Blackrock's return to Nagchaw.

During Jason's last self-imposed exile, his mother, ShuShu Blackrock, had passed away. She passed with deep regrets about being unable to convince her son to return to Nagchaw. The Nagchaw elders understood that while in-training, this young medicine man crossed into the spirit world and witnessed a horrific past life atrocity as a boarding school child. His re-traumatization was at the heart of his spiraling out of control and led to his leaving Nagchaw Nation twice and the last time was for well over a decade.

"What is Jason Blackrock doing back here after running away to Sierra Vista. I heard that he made buckets of money telling fortunes to vacationing tourists. What reason does he have to return and stir things up by bringing his hocus pocus to Nagchaw?" Councilman Lewis asked.

"Okay, okay, I know that we're all concerned about his return. Especially because he's drawing in our young people, most of whom have never heard of him and are unaware of his past. Still, Jason is one of us and he deserves a chance to redeem himself. We only know secondhand of his activities, so I prefer that we not judge and convict him based on rumors. I'm considering going out to see him to find out what his intentions are, and I'll report back to you after I've done that," Stevie said.

"I'd like to go with you if you don't mind. Grandma Moon has an extensive history with him, and she's talked with me at length about their time together and why she felt he made the decision to leave Nagchaw Nation," I said.

"Sure Jos, it might be helpful if you are there. I don't want our visit to come off as a judge and jury scenario ready to convict him. I'd like to open the door to discussing why he's returned without creating any animosity," Stevie said.

"I agree. I think he's already been through so much. I want to be sensitive to the suffering that drove him to turn his back on those who love him and live in a state of self-imposed exile," I said.

"Jos, after we finish here, let's look at our schedules and see when we can go out to see him. I understand that he's set up camp about forty-five minutes from here at Crystal Mountain Ridge," Stevie said.

The meeting ended after a flurry of discussion about the need for clarification around Jason's return and his intentions for holding his "visioning sessions" with the Nagchaw youth.

"Stevie, I can go whenever it is most convenient for you. There's nothing on my calendar that can't be rescheduled without issue," I said.

"Okay, good, then let's go in a couple of days, how about on Friday? That gives us some time to decide what questions we'll have for him. We can also send a written notice to him by way of a Tribal Carrier."

"A Tribal Carrier?" I asked.

"Yes, it's our modern-day version of the Pony Express. With a few of our elders who refuse to get phones, that's how we communicate with them, if there's no family member we can go through," Stevie said.

"Okay, that's a great idea. That way Jason won't feel like we're jumping out at him without any notice."

"Jos, would you please do a rough draft of the notice before I have Rachael type it up on Tribal Stationary?" Stevie asked.

"Yes, I'd like to do that. I think the wording needs to be clear so that there's no confusion about our intentions," I said.

"Absolutely, I'd like to avoid any suspicion of ill will on our part," Stevie said.

When Friday arrived, I was nervous about taking our trip out to Jason's camp. We left at the crack of dawn to avoid the worst of the heat and took Stevie's El Camino, which had better AC than my Chevy Cavalier Coupe. We each brought a water jug for the trip since there is not much out by Crystal Mountain Ridge. The drive went quickly, the early morning weather was slightly warm but comfortable, and we weren't sure what to expect.

We easily found Jason's roadside camp just off the reservation at an RV hook up station. His state-of-the-art motorhome with a pop-up roof was parked under Blue Palo Verde trees which offered additional shade. After hearing us drive up, Jason came outside.

"A'ho, Jason, kamdothk muuvaam 'nyyuu 'diik." (Hello, Jason, we came to see how you are doing), Stevie said.

"Yes, I received your notice. Thanks for sending it so that I'd not miss your arrival," Jason said.

"Your motorhome looks to be fully equipped," Stevie said.

"Yes, it is. I got a real deal on this from a tourist who was buying a new one, lucky me! It has a small kitchen, heated water, air conditioning, and a portable toilet and shower. All the conveniences of home away from home. Please come in," Jason said.

We entered and found his home to be modestly furnished with Indigenous art on the walls and the scent of sage lingering in the air. He motioned for us to take a seat on a Mission-style wood framed sofa covered with a sage, rust, and brown Pendleton blanket. Jason brought us both a glass of iced sun tea, which we eagerly drank.

"Jason, we wanted to come and see you after hearing that you'd returned to Nagchaw. I wanted to see how you were and to check-in with what's going on out here," Stevie said.

"Your return has been a surprise for many. We'd love to hear about how you are doing and what your plans are now that you're back," I said.

"Yes, as you stated in your written notice. I'm sure many were surprised to hear that I'd come back. I've been gone for a long time, and much has happened for me," Jason said.

"It sounds like things might be different for you now. What made you decide to return," I asked.

"Yes, my life has changed, for the better. I had to work through the trauma I'd experience, which Grandma Moon warned me about before I went off the rails," Jason said.

"How were you able to do that? I mean, who was there to help you with that? I can't imagine that you had to deal with that atrocity alone," I said.

"No, you're right, I couldn't have done it alone. While in Sierra Vista I met a Cocopah man, who was also a trained crisis counselor. He and I met regularly for a few years. His connection and understanding of First Nations history, along with this crisis training helped me immensely. I'm no longer possessed by what happened to me," Jason said.

"That's fantastic, Jason. I know Grandma Moon will be so happy to hear about this, if you don't mind that I tell her," I said.

"No, of course not, she's been nothing but good to me my entire life. I owe her so much, and I need to see her and Pawpaw to ask for their forgiveness. Early on they came to Sierra Vista after I left, but I refused to see them. I was drinking heavily and filled with shame. I couldn't face them," Jason said.

"Yes, go see them, Jason. They've never forgotten about you. I know she and Pawpaw remember you in their daily prayers and rituals," I said.

At that moment, Jason got up and took what looked to be a hand carved bamboo flute off a shelf and asked if he could play for us. The enticing melody lasted a couple of minutes before he stopped.

"Thank you, Jason, that was beautiful."

"You're welcome, I play often now. The melody just comes out of me. When I was in the depths of my trauma, I lost my ability to hear the music. This was how I knew that healing had taken place. I was able to play my flute again. I can hear a spontaneous melody and play at will," Jason said.

We sat in silence as Jason took our glasses and refilled them with sun tea. When he returned, Stevie changed the direction of our conversation.

"So, Jason, we've heard that you're holding visioning sessions with some of the Nagchaw youth," Stevie said.

"Yes, I am. You know I wasn't much older than the youngsters I've seen. I know what that search for meaning is like. You have questions about what your clan elders tell you, and that's not about disrespecting them, but questioning what things mean. Understanding goes beyond knowing about the history of rituals, so that's what I'm doing when given the opportunity," Jason said.

"Are you saying that there can be a disconnect between knowing the rituals and their histories with what the deeper spiritual connection might be?" I asked.

"In a nutshell, yes. The modern world doesn't understand the basis of our traditions or rituals and tends to label them as myths, which invalidates them. My visioning work with the youth is about connecting the dots, answering their questions, if I can, and helping them see a path forward for their future. Being able to live between two worlds, is not an easy thing to do," Jason said.

"So, you aren't telling fortunes or predicting their futures?" Stevie asked.

"No, I am not. When I get a strong impression or can see something that might present in their future, I speak about the energetic aspect of that condition or experience without labeling it. This way it doesn't become something set in stone, and their future remains malleable," Jason said.

At that moment Stevie and I looked at each other as if we shared the same thought; Klay's workshop might be an opportunity for integrating what Jason is doing with the youth.

"You know Jason, we're about to start a workshop series for Nagchaw youth titled *Exploring the Ancients Universe and Beyond* with a former high school science teacher named Klay Swiftwater," Stevie said.

"Yes, Klay wants to integrate the customs, rituals, and ways of the Nagchaw Ancients with modern day science in such a manner that the two viewpoints are integrated and complimentary," I said.

"Yes, that sounds like what I'm doing but on a small more personal scale by providing a context for living between two worlds," Jason said.

"Jason, would you be open to meeting Klay, discussing his workshop series, and sharing what you've been doing in your visioning sessions with him? The purpose of this meeting would be to see if there might be a way to integrate into the workshop what you're doing," I said.

"Whoa, that's a big step. I would have to think about this and pray about it," Jason said.

"Of course, I understand," I said.

"Take as long as you need to decide if this is something you might consider or feel called to do," Stevie said.

"Meeting to discuss this possibility is no commitment. You might not feel like you and Klay mesh well. He's an intellectual type, so your personalities and orientations are like the two sides of a coin," I said.

"Well, you can't have a coin without two sides, now can you?"

We all laughed. Jason seemed relaxed and in good spirits after our two-hour conversation.

Stevie said that he needed to get back to the Tribal Council office.

"Jason, thank you so much for meeting with us. I'm happy to have you back home and hearing about your personal journey is great news," Stevie said.

"Yes, Jason, I'm glad to have you back too. Grandma Moon and Pawpaw will be so happy to hear of our visit," I said.

"Oh, so, you didn't mention that you were coming out today?" Jason asked.

"No, I didn't. I thought I'd wait until after our meeting because I knew she would have insisted on coming with us," I said.

"Yes, I'm sure she would have," Jason chuckled.

"Jason, please come by the Tribal Council office or call me once you decide either way. If you are interested, we'll have to present the idea of a meeting between you two and see what Klay says," Stevie said.

"Yes, and please, there's no pressure on you to do this. Although we believe your contribution would enrich the workshop series, the decision about your participation is completely yours," I said.

"Ayuu nymuuaay dany 'iiwaa xotk" (for what you give me-my heart is good) – Jason said.

CHAPTER 10

Blending World Views

*"The transition process is really a loop in the life-jour-
ney, a going out and away from the main flow for a
time and then coming around and back. The neutral
zone is meant to be only a temporary state. It is,
as they say, a great place to visit, but you wouldn't
want to live there. When the neutral zone has done
its work, you come back. Socially, this means that
the isolated person returns from the disengaged
state and the wilderness to set about translating
insight and idea into action and form."*

~ William Bridges, from *Transitions: Making
Sense of Life's Changes*

We left Crystal Mountain Ridge elated after
a heartfelt meeting, which was more than
either of us had expected. I knew that Klay might
need some convincing about working with Jason.
I decided that Stevie and I should do some preparation before asking Klay.

"So, what do you think, Jos? Will Klay be open
to meeting with Jason?" Stevie asked.

"I'm not sure, Klay's used to soloing it, and he
might be apprehensive about sharing the stage.

On the other hand, he just might be open to the idea," I said.

"Well, let me call him and tell him that we'd like to meet. I think the request coming from me will make him less likely to reject the idea right away," Stevie said.

"When will you call him?" I asked.

"After we get back this afternoon," Stevie said.

"I'm free on Monday. Can we meet then?" I asked.

"Yes, Monday morning works for me too," Stevie said.

On Monday morning, Stevie and I met in his office with Klay and gave him an overview of our visit to Crystal Mountain Ridge. We presented the idea of the two men meeting to see if working together might be an option.

"Yes, I can see why you'd consider this for the workshop series. I could rearrange the curriculum so that his contributions fit into the material being covered. That's far less of an issue than seeing if we're able to work well as a unit," Klay said.

"That's exactly why we thought scheduling a meeting with the two of you would be a good idea," Stevie said.

"Yes, this way you both could learn about one another and get more familiar with where you each were coming from as far as your frame of reference goes," I said.

"Absolutely, there's no way to skip this meeting

because without knowing if we'd be able to work together, it's really a pointless conversation. We'd also need to have clarification on his role as it relates to mine," Klay said.

"Yes, Jason would be a contracted guest presenter throughout the series. He'd be a co-fa-cilitator, but it's your workshop Klay. You will have full responsibility for the series, but Jason will have a significant and complimentary role. You might say that his presentations will be the icing on the cake," I said.

"Well, we all know that any good cake needs icing to hit the spot," Klay said.

"Okay, good, I just heard back from Jason late Friday. He's interested in meeting with you Klay, to explore the possibility of working together," Stevie said.

"So, how about meeting with him in my office on Wednesday afternoon or Thursday morning," I asked.

"Wednesday afternoon works for me," Klay said.

"Okay, that works for me too. I'll send out a Tribal Carrier to notify Jason," Stevie said.

The meeting between Klay and Jason was more successful than Stevie or I ever thought it would be. After introductions, the first part of the meeting was an overview of Exploring the Ancients Universe and Beyond workshop. Stevie stated that we hoped that they would find a way so that working together their efforts would enrich the program. Then we left the two of them alone to speak further about how their two perspectives could mesh for an enriched workshop experience and what their partnership might become. Then we asked to reconvene after they'd finished to hear their thoughts. Some thirty minutes later, we were notified that they were ready to reconvene.

"It is my hope that blending Western scientific principles and the wisdom of the Nagchaw Ancients will open the door to the potential power of each youth to improve not only their life but the world around them. The experiments and materials covered will support an openness to seeing the wholeness of two historically separate traditions," Klay said.

"Yes, understanding how the teachings of the Nagchaw Ancients are not contrary to basic scientific beliefs will allow the youth to experience a dimension of wholeness that is the source of our true nature. I believe that the workshop will show how in each moment we can use our power to deepen our understanding of the Universe. This experience will honor traveling the path of the Red Road by integrating the ways of the Nagchaw Ancients. As a result, a new appreciation of their traditions and teachings will be nurtured," Jason said.

The wrap up discussion continued with Stevie and I asking occasional questions. Klay and Jason seemed excited and eager to tackle this ambitious project. Stevie and I met afterwards to assess the outcome and could hardly contain our laughter about the concerns we had prior to this meeting taking place.

"Gosh, we were more than a little off base in thinking that this might not go well." Stevie said.

"Yes, I was apprehensive about these two being able to find any common ground as individuals. Although we were not privy to their personal exchange, I am guessing they wouldn't have presented so enthusiastically about working together had it not gone well," I said.

"I believe that to be an accurate assessment, Ms. Gentry," Stevie said.

"Stevie, how about the rest of the council members? Will you get any push back from them about Jason's return and being involved with Klay's workshop?" I asked.

"Oh, more than likely, but I've already drafted an email giving them an overview of our two-hour visit with Jason. If you'd like to include a section about the joining of forces for the workshop series, I'll add that. The email will be from both of us and will state if there are any concerns they'll be addressed at the next council meeting," Stevie said.

Over the next couple of months, Klay and Jason started meeting regularly. Stevie had a table, chairs, and two desks moved into an unused room downstairs. Jason had moved his motorhome to Nagchaw and was able to walk to the cultural center and tribal offices. Although these two men had vastly different personalities, they seemed to relate well. It warmed my heart to periodically hear them laughing as they passed through the downstairs lobby.

The council members who had concerns about Jason's return were quelled. They had accepted that Jason had healed and would be instrumental in the contributions he would make to Exploring the Ancients Universe and Beyond workshop.

The Tribal Voice ran a Special Edition covering the workshop series and information on how to sign up. The edition had color pictures and gave an overview of both men's background related to having longstanding indigenous roots. Klay's background in secondary education as a science teacher was highlighted along with the mention of his running of the college prep program at Flagstaff High School. Jason's introduction mentioned his Blackrock clan and the fact that he came from an extensive line of gifted generational Medicine Men. Mention was also made of his connection to the Yellowbird clan by way of Grandma Moon and Pawpaw.

The Tribal Voice Special Edition was exceptionally well done. The Coleman Board of Education got wind of the series and reached out asking to be updated about the outcome as a courtesy. Apparently, Coleman high school had been subjected to a state board of education review. Their school curriculum was dinged for not being inclusive enough where other cultural viewpoints were concerned. In response to the school board's request, I notified them that I would send a letter at the conclusion of the first workshop series. Then, I let Klay and Jason know about the request and asked them to provide me with an overview of series highlights.

Life was good, things were cruising along; the Tribal Council had filled their open seat and were busy attending to the needs of the tribe with what seemed like never-ending challenges, projects, and potential business opportunities.

I couldn't have been happier with the range of creativity showcased. The history, culture, traditions, music, and art of the Nagchaw Nation as well as the language and educational components made for an impressive compilation. There were exhibits featuring artifacts, tools, baskets, woven blankets, ceremonial clothing, and jewelry as well as a special section featuring powwows, sweats, drumming, and healing circles.

In addition, there were language classes taught by Lucy Keeton who was reintroducing the

Uto-Aztecan language. The icing on the cake was Klay Swiftwater and Jason Blackrock's combined efforts with the Exploring the Ancients Universe workshop series. In fact, things were going so well that National Geographic had reached out and asked to do a cultural exposé for their upcoming Honoring First Nations edition.

Although Stevie and I both recognized that there was something special between us, with so much happening at work, the development of our relationship got moved to the back burner. More specifically, I was sure that Stevie wanted to pursue a full-fledged relationship, but I still had fears about venturing into what felt like deep waters.

CHAPTER 11

Two Hearts Beat as One

"Genuine beginnings begin within us, even when they are brought to our attention by external opportunities. It is out of the formlessness of the neutral zone that the new form emerges and out of the barrenness of the fallow time that new life springs. Yes, until you are ready, you probably won't make a real beginning."

~ William Bridges, from *Transitions: Making Sense of Life's Changes*

I had been so busy that I'd hardly had time to ponder the possibility of furthering my relationship with Stevie outside of work. Truthfully, I wasn't ready, until now, and Stevie had been waiting for the right time to make his move.

We had decided to go to dinner in Coleman at Cattleman's Steakhouse that Saturday evening. When he picked me up, I sensed a more intense energy than normal and wondered what he was up to. After placing our dinner order, Stevie wasn't saying much, which worried me. Then, my worries melted away as he took my hand, looked into my eyes, and spoke.

"Joslin, I've had you on my mind a lot lately, and I've missed our time together away from work. I know working together complicates things, but I don't want to ignore what I know and feel for you because of that. I've thought about what the future with you would be like, and I want that future. I know that you feel something for me too, and I see no good reason why we can't make a go of it as a couple," Stevie said.

I was stunned, although I couldn't disagree. I was speechless, as well as elated. It took a few seconds to collect myself enough to speak coherently.

"Yes, Stevie, I feel something special for you too. You are such a good man. I trust you and I know that you would not intentionally do anything to hurt me," I said.

"A girlfriend is good enough for kids, Jos, but I was thinking more like a fiancée and within a reasonable time, you'd be my wife," Stevie said.

Once again, I was stunned and needed to take a few seconds to collect myself before speaking.

"Fiancée, so soon? Really?" I asked.

"Yes, I don't think we'd need to announce anything to anyone right off. As soon as it's known that we're officially engaged, I'm sure the word will get around that a commitment ceremony would be around the corner," Stevie said.

"Jos, I know enough about you to skip the dating stage. Besides, I'm beyond wanting a girlfriend. I want us to look to the future, to build a stable, committed relationship, and yes, marrying at some point," Stevie said.

"But Stevie, appearances are important given the roles we have; so, could we please start with the boyfriend-girlfriend stage before moving into being fiancées?" I asked.

"Yes Ma'am, we can do that if that makes you more comfortable. I know that dating is how things usually start. It's the getting to know one another stage, but we've had the advantage of working together for almost three years which has allowed us to see each other in a more in-depth manner," Stevie said.

"In all honesty, I've had dreams about us together, and the thought of being with you makes me happy," I said.

"Well, good. I see us married within a reasonable time, Joslin," Stevie said as he reached into his jacket pocket and pulled out a small muslin sack with sage green ribbon threading the opening. "Joslin, this is something that's been in my family a long time, and I'd like you to have it," Stevie said handing the sack to me.

As I pulled the sage green ribbon, I reached in and pulled out a beautiful silver and turquoise bracelet. I took the bracelet and put it around my wrist with my other bracelets. They looked like a matching set, and it warmed my heart that he gave it to me. It was his mother's bracelet. I'd noticed it on her wrist in several pictures.

"Thank you, Stevie, it's beautiful. It's an old bracelet, I can tell by the silver work," I said.

"It looks beautiful on you, Jos. It was my mother's favorite bracelet. She wore it daily. It was the one thing I wanted after she passed. It reminds me of being loved by her. It makes sense to me that you should wear it now," Stevie said.

Knowing this filled my heart as I leaned across the table and kissed him. At that moment, I heard Keith's voice, '*Sister, you are on the road to many blessings*', and I couldn't help but smile.

In what seemed like a blink of an eye, six months passed, and our engagement was announced at a mid-summer intertribal powwow. Stevie was determined that we be married in late October, which meant that our engagement would be even shorter than our so-called dating period. The news was received with joy and an exuberance that I hadn't fully expected. This acceptance and joy helped quell any fears that would occasionally pop up around thoughts of being in a committed relationship and married. I was aware that my once deep-seated fear of intimacy had started to thaw, which meant that I was healing from the trauma of my upbringing.

As the summer neared its end, I wondered about inviting Sam, my father. Although our commitment ceremony wouldn't be a traditional wedding ceremony, we would be legally married, and I still felt obligated to invite my father.

"Daughter, you do not have to do anything you don't want to. You know you can send Sam a postnuptial announcement," Mom said.

"Yes, I could do that. As much as I'm uncertain about inviting him, I still wonder if he'd like to attend," I said.

"I can't help you there. All I know is that since we've moved to Nagchaw, he hasn't made any effort to reach out to you, has he?" Mom asked.

"No, he hasn't, but should that be the determining factor?" I asked.

"Oh Jos, that's completely up to you," Mom said.

"I could invite him and ask that he let me know as soon as possible," I said.

"You aren't thinking of having Sam walk you down the aisle, are you?" Mom asked.

"Stevie and I want a traditional Nagchaw commitment ceremony, but we both thought that it would be appropriate to honor the other side of our heritage by having my father walk me down the aisle," I said.

"Well, Jos, Pawpaw would be more than willing to do that for you," Mom said.

"Yes, I know he would, and both Stevie and I would be honored to have him do that. Still, you realize that there'd be no discussion about who would walk me down the aisle, if my brother was here. Keith would be the one to do that," I said.

"I know honey, and your brother would have been elated to walk you down the aisle too. As far as your father goes, just be sure to give him a deadline by which to let you know of his plans. Your father was always good about keeping his deadlines," Mom said.

Taking to heart Mom's comment, I mailed a card with a note to Sam stating that I would be married to Stevie Bahe and that it would be a traditional Nagchaw ceremony. I stated that if he would like to attend, I would welcome his presence and would ask that he walk me down the aisle. Either way, I ask that he let me know as early as possible so that I could plan accordingly.

Sam's handwritten reply arrived two weeks later inside a congratulations on your marriage card. It included a check with the notation: For the wedding. He wished Stevie and I well and stated that he felt that it would not be appropriate for him to attend our wedding given all that had happened. I wasn't really surprised, and I was relieved that I had asked and given him an opportunity to decide if he wanted to attend. Now I could move forward with what felt to be the most appropriate decision, and I knew Pawpaw would be delighted to walk me down the aisle.

Because both the Yellowbird and Bahe extended clans were a good size, we decided to hold our commitment ceremony in the Tribal Council's Special Events Room. Once we'd announced the Saturday, October 26th, wedding date, Mom and Grandma Moon got busy planning the food and drink. We asked that there be a combination of traditional and modern food served, representing the blended backgrounds that Stevie and I were from. We also asked that Pawpaw's plum and apricot wine be served for the toast. Stevie and I couldn't decide which traditional commitment rituals we wanted, so we combined a few of them. Stevie's father offered the handmade, intricately decorated two spout Wedding Vessel that he and Lily used. Always one step ahead, Grandma Moon had made my Wedding Blanket after Mom and I moved back to Nagchaw, so it would finally come out of the storage trunk.

I wanted my wedding dress to be a traditional Nagchaw design, which meant it would be made of woven sage green cloth trimmed with beaded leather, jingle bells, and feathers in my other favorite colors rust with silver trim. Stevie decided that his clothing would be of the same colors so that it would reflect our being of like mind. We each wore a special piece of jewelry that we gave each other. I wore the silver and turquoise bracelet that he'd given me when he told me he wanted us to marry. He wore a beaded leather bolero with a medicine wheel center that I'd created for him in our wedding colors.

We asked Mike Milton and the Thunder Road drumming group to perform at the beginning of the ceremony as Pawpaw walked me down the aisle. Then we asked Jason Blackrock to play his hand carved bamboo flute as we asked Great Spirit to bless our union. Then we spoke our marriage promises to each other which united our clans. Finally, we closed our ceremony by drinking Pawpaw's plum and apricot wine from the two spout Wedding Vessel and then Mom and Jericho wrapped us in our Wedding Blanket.

Finally, The Tribal Voice covered our ceremony, which was published with pictures and made available for all to see. I mailed a copy of that Special Edition to Dad. I included a short note stating that I held no resentment about his decision not to attend our wedding.

As happy as I was that this had all come to fruition, I couldn't help but feel a little sad that Keith wasn't present. He would have been pleased that Stevie and I were marrying.

CHAPTER 12

Coming Full Circle

"It is good to grow deep roots within our community and that means that we must go deep into ourselves and deep into our commitment to being on a spiritual path."

~ Doug Good Feather, from *Think Indigenous*

The years after our commitment ceremony were filled with rich and rewarding experiences. Make no mistake, there have also been challenges, along with the occasional heart break. Still, what these experiences have taught me is that my worst enemy is the conversation that goes on between my ears. Life moves in cycles, things appear to fall apart and come back together again. Being sucked into believing that there's never enough leaves you constantly on the hunt.

I finished another three years as the Director of the Nagchaw Cultural Center then Klay Swiftwater got his wish and took over my position. The transition was as smooth as silk.

In fact, due to the overwhelming response to the National Geographic First Nations edition, Klay and Jason were given an Honorary Carl Sagen Award. Their creative, culturally diverse programming by way of Exploring the Ancients Universe and Beyond was touted as a first-rate example of blending Western scientific principles and indigenous spirituality to support a wholistic perspective.

In addition, Jason Blackrock reconnected with Grandma Moon and Pawpaw and mended what needed mending. Little by little Jason moved into position to carry the load that Grandma Moon had been carrying as the Nagchaw Medicine Woman for many years. He was now more than ever ready to be the primary Nagchaw Medicine Man that he was always meant to be.

There were not just new beginnings during these years, there were also endings. Pawpaw was the first to leave us and when that time came Mom and Grandma took care of the preparations. Pawpaw's body was ritually cleansed and then dressed in his favorite regalia before being placed on a woven grass mat on the funeral pyre. Jason lit the fire as the Thunder Road group drummed and sang. And just as had happened with Keith's final ceremony, I looked to the sky and saw a brown eagle soaring above waiting to escort Pawpaw's soul to the heavens to be with the Nagchaw Ancients.

Shortly after Pawpaw passed, Mom and Jericho Jefferson married in a small private ceremony at his home. Both admitted that they'd wanted to do this for a while but decided to wait until after our commitment ceremony.

Stevie and I designed and built an adobe-style home before we became parents of a beautiful little boy we named Keith. As he grew, we were amazed at how much he looked like the uncle he shared a name with. Two years later, we were blessed with a little sister for Keith, Lily. Our family filled my heart with more joy than I ever knew possible. Stevie was at home in his role as a father and found great joy in caring and providing for me and his children. He continued as the Nagchaw Tribal Chief Executive for an additional decade before opening a small handyman business on Nagchaw Central.

Our Keith and Lily grew up to be fine people. They both finished their educations with Keith getting my creative gene and becoming an artist. He displayed his work on Nagchaw at the cultural center and at the Phoenix and Tucson Art Gallery where he sold most of his paintings. Lily went on to medical school and became a Nurse Practitioner at the Native American Health Center. Having specialized in substance abuse treatment, she worked side by side with Mike Milton in the Thunder Road Recovery program. In the lobby area at the entrance to her clinic space, she had her father create a handmade sign which read:

Remember no matter where you've been or what you've done, you are just one decision away from a different life.

I know that there will be many more good times, as well as challenges. I read somewhere that our passion once discovered is at the heart of our life's purpose. What fills our hearts with joy is very likely the gift that's been with us through many lifetime journeys. When we share our gift with others, it will be reflected in the manner with which we walk in this world on the Red Road.

As I sit in my rocking chair on this porch, I am an old woman who can look back and see the truth of my journey. My wish for you? That you find a path with heart that allows you to look back at where you've come from and realize how blessed you are.

The End

About the Author

Toni was born in San Antonio, Texas, on April 20th while her father was stationed at Lackland Air Force Base. Raised as a Roman Catholic, she was the firstborn of eight, seven girls and a boy. Her bicultural background references her Mexican American father and her mother of European descent. Most of her immediate family lives in Arizona.

She graduated from the undergraduate School of Social Work at Arizona State University and then from the Graduate School of Holistic Studies at John F. Kennedy University in Northern California. Her career has been in the nonprofit Health and Human Services arena, working with multiple underserved populations. Early in her career, she worked with a Pima population from the Gila River Indian Reservation south of Chandler, Arizona.

Toni is a twice-published poet and *Coming Full Circle* is the third book of the *Between Two Worlds Series.* She's recently retired and lives in Oakland, California with her long-term softball playing partner, Rick, and their cat, Coco. #CatTownRocks

OTHER BOOKS BY TONI TARANGO

The *Between Two Worlds Series:*
    As the Twig is Bent
    As the Eagle Soars
    Coming Full Circle

www.ingramcontent.com/pod-product-compliance
Lightning Source LLC
Chambersburg PA
CBHW020414130626
46549CB00006B/2552